SEARCHING FOR GRACE

BY JACKIE JORDAN

Searching for Grace

Jordan, Jackie
ISBN 978-0-578-32911-6 (Paperback)
ISBN 978-0-578-32912-3 (eBook)

Edited by IM Writing
Book production and cover design by Publish and Promote.
Interior layout and design by Perseus Design.
Printed and bound in the USA.

Note to the reader: This is a work of fiction. Unless otherwise indicated, all the names, characters, businesses, places, events, and incidents in this book are either the product of the author's imagination or used in a fictitious manner. Any resemblance to actual persons, living or dead, or actual events is purely coincidental. The information is provided for educational purposes only. In the event you use any of the information in this book for yourself, which is your constitutional right, the author and publisher assume no responsibility for your actions.

Amazing Grace

John Newton
1772

Amazing grace, how sweet the sound,
That saved a wretch like me!
I once was lost, but now am found,
Was blind, but now I see.

. . .

Through many dangers, toils and snares
I have already come;
'Tis grace has brought me safe thus far,
and grace will lead me home.

CONTENTS

INTRODUCTION

This book grew out of my lifelong interest in the genealogy of my African American family. Research that started out as a hobby became a passion. Initially, I was satisfied with creating elaborate family reunion charts with rectangles and connecting lines that dispassionately displayed relationships among individuals. I looked through national and state electronic records and visited state archives, county courthouses, and local libraries, searching for documents about my ancestors and the white people who had enslaved them. It took me years to realize that my work produced genealogy charts with names and dates but that lacked historical contexts to understand the individuals in the boxes.

I was surprised how often I thought and cared about my ancestors, some of whom I knew only by name. I wanted to put "flesh to dry bones" by supplementing my research with historical data, family history, frequent trips to revisit familiar family sites, and memories of my own experiences growing up in Phenix City, Alabama. My ancestors figuratively came alive. What facts I could never possibly know,

I gave myself permission to imagine and to create new characters and events in their lives.

My trips to Africa gave me a different lens to see and define myself. I am a descendant of the Yoruba people of Nigeria and the Tikars in Cameroon. The Yorubas and Tikars were captured by Europeans, chained, and tightly packed below the decks of ships where they suffered indescribable pain and abuse. They arrived on the shores of America two months after leaving their homelands, barely alive but not broken. No European trader of human beings, Alabama or Georgia enslaver, or Jim Crow law could crush or harness my family's resilience and fortitude.

This is a tribute to my enslaved great-great grand parents, James and Harriett and Giles and Julia Jordan, my grandparents Rev. Robert and Rosie Lee Harris, and my parents Eddie and Sarah Harris Jordan. The book is dedicated to my late husband, Dr. Russell W. Irvine (1944-2018) – my lover, friend, and intellectual partner for fifty years. There will never be a day when I don't think of him and wish he were by my side.

The book would not be possible without the assistance and support of my family and friends. Thanks to my daughter, Kelli Irvine Neptune, and my sisters: Pat Van Dyke, Angela J. Davis, and especially Jennifer Jordan, who encouraged and pushed me to be a better writer. My friends, Vanessa Siddle Walker and Miriam Reid gave me excellent ideas for the storyline. Thanks to Janell Walden Agyeman, Founder of Next Steps Literary Services, and Editor Cheryl Odeyele for their patience, wise advice, and guidance throughout this process.

CHAPTER ONE

WASHINGTON, DC

When Neema Washington graduated from high school in Nashville in 1966, everybody assumed she would enroll at Fisk University. It was her parents' alma mater, and she had grown up on the campus. Most importantly, Neema could attend Fisk tuition-free because her mother, Lily Robinson Washington, worked there. Who could argue against free college?

But Neema had another idea, and when it came time to apply to colleges, she told her parents that she wanted to leave Nashville and go to Howard University in Washington, DC. They reacted as if their daughter wanted to enroll at the University of Sodom and Gomorrah. Her father, Rev. Joseph Washington, paced the room, quietly asking God why his child would want to do such a thing. Fisk's motto was, "Her sons and daughters are ever at the altar," and so he and Lily believed that Fisk offered a more wholesome, Christian environment than Howard.

Lily was anxious over the fact that she was losing control of her daughter's life and near tears. In an overly emotional delivery that was a bit out of character, she stated her case.

"Howard is too big, too far, too expensive. DC is too dangerous, and full of too many big-city northern students without proper Christian upbringings."

Neema didn't know why her parents were so adamantly against her going to Howard, and the reason would be decades in coming. The tension in the Washington home that January of 1966 blanketed the atmosphere like an African monsoon.

Joseph asked repeatedly, "Have you lost your mind? Are you following some boy to Howard? Do you realize how much money we could save for your graduate school if you went to Fisk?"

But Neema was adamant in her decision, and so her parents gave her permission to apply to both Fisk and Howard. Neema was elated over the possibility that she might attend the college of her dreams.

The acceptance letter from Fisk arrived in March. By April, with no communication from Howard, Joseph and Lily were delighted by the prospect of their daughter attending their alma mater and couldn't help but secretly gloat. Deeply disappointed, Neema resigned herself to staying in Nashville.

April was almost over when Neema finally received an answer from Howard. She had been accepted! In fact, she had earned a full-ride – tuition, room and board, and books. She could not believe her good fortune. Her parents, on the other hand, were both shocked and disappointed. They never imagined that she would get a scholarship package that matched the Fisk benefits.

With money she had saved from a part-time summer job, Neema bought her train ticket and boarded the train for DC on August 15, 1966. As she watched other college-bound students board with their parents who were accompanying them to the beginning of their new lives, Neema began to feel her self-confidence dissipating. She tried to look happy as she waved goodbye to her parents through the train window, but she felt alone and scared. Lily was dabbing her eyes, and Joseph waved back with a pained, crooked smile. The older woman sitting next to Neema was snoring before they left the terminal. What the hell, she wondered, have I gotten myself into?

Neema used the long overnight train ride to think about her future. Finally, she was going someplace where no one knew her parents. She would meet new people and find her own way, free to re-make herself. Exactly who that new person might be she didn't know, but she had the time and space to figure it out.

* * * * *

Neema had never visited Howard University before she got out of the cab in front of the women's dormitories, Tubman Quadrangle. She entered the imposing structure through the single entrance that led to five connected dorms – Baldwin, Truth, Frazier, Crandall, Wheatley – that surrounded a courtyard. Neema took her place at the end of the long check-in line and waited her turn. When Neema reached the counter, an overzealous student assistant requested her name, dorm, and room number. "Neema Washington, 305 Truth Hall," she said.

While Neema was completing the required forms, a stern, very tall, large-built woman exited an office behind the counter. Holding her keys in one hand and purse in the other, she flashed what looked like a phony grin.

"Hello, young ladies. I am Dean Owens, the Dean of Women."

Having been around the staff and faculty of Fisk for years, Neema knew that Dean Owens's responsibilities would include enforcing the 11:00 p.m. curfew, monitoring student conduct, and, most importantly and improbably, protecting the chastity of women students.

"I am extremely honored to welcome you to Howard University," she continued, "and specifically to what we call the Quad family. You are about to embark upon a life-changing experience and become a Howard woman. I know you will carry yourself with grace and dignity. If you need anything, my staff is here twenty-four hours a day, seven days a week. I will give you an official welcome this week."

Dean Owens finished and stood there with a frozen smile. The confused students looked at each other. Fortunately, one astute young woman started clapping and was quickly joined by the others. Dean Owens smiled, thanked the group, and left. Neema was given a key and some complicated instructions on how to find her room through the underground tunnels. Apparently looking lost, she was rescued by a student resident advisor.

"Where are you going? These tunnels can be confusing the first week or so. Here, let me help carry one of your suitcases."

Neema followed the helpful student who pointed to various points of interest.

"This is where you store your luggage. The laundry room is on your right. If you lived in Wheatley, you'd take these sets of elevators, but let's keep going. Baldwin Hall is on the left, but we're going straight ahead."

Neema's head was swimming. Finally, the student pointed to the elevator to Truth Hall.

"Hope to see you around," she said as she waved Neema on. "Good luck."

Neema pushed her key into the keyhole of 305 Truth, but the door was not fully shut and so it swung open. To her surprise, she saw that she had not one but two roommates. Howard hadn't informed her of its new three-person per room housing policy for freshmen. Neema felt annoyed but tried not to show it.

Her two roommates introduced themselves. Tracy, who preferred to be called Twinky, was from Los Angeles. She was sprawled across the only single bed, which was partially buried under a pile of clothing. Neema didn't want to stare, but she was mesmerized by Twinky's red hair. She was used to seeing older Black women with dyed black hair or a blue rinse and knew plenty of light-skinned Black girls with freckles and light-colored hair. But she had never seen a dark-skinned teenager with dyed red hair.

Her other roommate, Donna was from New York City. She was busy organizing one of the room's two desks and had claimed the lower bunk, leaving the top bunk bed for Neema. She offered to share the closet and asked Twinky if she would share the other desk. Neema found Twinky's chilly response disconcerting: "We'll do what we have to do."

Neema felt like crying. Instead of starting to unpack her bags, she sat in one of the uncomfortable desk chairs and tried to compose herself. When she stopped feeling sorry for herself, she concluded that she had few options. Returning home was not one of them.

Her first night in Tubman Quad was a disaster. By midnight, with much effort and negotiation, 305 Truth Hall was habitable. Neema had squeezed her belongings into every available space, including some makeshift cubbies she made from discarded cardboard boxes. Exhausted and a bit depressed, she climbed the five-slat ladder to her bed, lay on the hard six-inch mattress, and tried to fall asleep, but there was too much chatter and traffic in the hallway. She stared at the ceiling just feet from her face and felt claustrophobic. She thought of turning onto her side but didn't out of fear she might fall. The hallway noise didn't stop until 1:00 a.m. when the resident advisor asked everyone to quiet down. By then, Twinky was snoring loudly, a nuisance that would continue through Neema's entire freshman year.

Early the next morning, Neema left her room to check out Howard's main campus. As she walked up a steep hill about a block from her dorm, she got her first glimpse of Founders Library, a magnificent and imposing four-story structure. She slowly opened the door and peeped in. Since no one stopped her, Neema explored. The main entrance led to a curved marble stairway with mahogany handrails and decorative iron balusters that led upstairs. Curved ceilings with lights illuminated detailed woodwork on the fireplace mantels, paneled doors, and arched windows. The Reference Room featured an impressive and intimidating centerpiece – an immense wooden card catalog of books and other reference materials that she couldn't wait to dive into.

Freshman Orientation was a bore. Each freshman was assigned to a group of twenty students led by an upperclassman "Campus Pal." For the next three days, Neema walked around with her group touring buildings she had already discovered on her own. Neema's Campus Pal was Jim, a braggadocious senior from Chicago. He immediately targeted an attractive woman in the group whom he wanted to impress. Instead of sticking to the required script, he kept diverting to stories about his fraternity, his Dean's List GPA, his new apartment, and his car. Showing what a "man about town" he was, he rattled off trivial information about "outta sight" off-campus restaurants, Hecht's and Woody's department stores, Waxie Maxie's Record Shop, and Rock Creek Park. Jim was oblivious to the group's collective frustration. They just wanted to know how to register for classes and process their financial aid. Long lines and lack of organization at registration was a Howard tradition, and the freshmen were eager for advice on how to avoid the pitfalls.

The most formidable and urgent task for all freshmen, however, was finding the right group to hang out with. Neema resigned herself to getting along with her roommates, but she had nothing in common with either. So, she considered her options among the complicated and often overlapping social cliques.

The students from DC usually lived at home and socialized with people they knew from the local high schools. International students, who were mostly older and from Africa and the Caribbean, lived off-campus and tended to interact mainly with each other. Fraternity and sorority members spent just about all their time with each other and partied together on weekends. Undergraduate students who were enrolled in the same schools and colleges, be it Fine Arts, Engineering, Architecture, Education, and Pharmacy, took classes together, studied together, and naturally socialized together.

None of these communities had impenetrable boundaries, but Neema was appalled by the tension between the Northerners and the Southerners. She hadn't been in her room a week before Twinky and Donna started to press her about her origins. As far as they were concerned, only two cities south of the Mason-Dixon Line deserved recognition, Atlanta and Miami.

"I've *never* heard anything *good* about Nashville," Twinky said. "One of my LA friends said she went down South to visit her grandmother, and some of the people down there had outdoor toilets. Is that true?"

"Some people do and some don't," Neema said, trying to be civil. "It depends."

"Well, did ya'll have one?"

Neema stared at Twinky. "No."

Donna acted like Neema was the only person on earth who had never been to New York City.

"Do you mean to tell me you have never seen a Broadway play, a show at the Apollo, walked around Times Square, or ridden the subway? Girl, what planet you from?"

The roommates had a big laugh at Neema's expense.

Neema learned the word that folks were using to describe students from the South – bamas. Derived from Alabama, *bama* was a derogatory term that denoted an unsophisticated, uneducated southern Black person. She first heard the term when one of her floormates from New Jersey said, "Did you all see that bama dude trying to hit on me on the Freshman Boat Ride? Why would I give him the time of day? That country Negro is definitely not ready for prime time!"

Neema soon put the issue of her intelligence to rest when her floormates compared their class schedules.

"Neema, where's your schedule? Let's see if you have classes with any of us. When do you take the English 101?"

Neema put her schedule on the desk. One student picked it up and gasped. "How did you get in the Honors Program?"

The typically chatty group fell silent.

"I guess my placement test scores were pretty high," Neema answered as she picked up her schedule and left the room. She didn't have the nerve to say what she was thinking – "What ya'll think of us bamas, now?"

It took a while, but Neema eventually found two women she enjoyed spending time with. Rose was from Hampton, Virginia and Faye from Savannah, Georgia. They were roommates and lived just a few doors down from Neema, who began to hang out in their room most of the time. They had a third roommate, but she usually spent her time in Crandall Hall with her high school friends from Cleveland.

The trio sat together in the cafeteria, figured out how to catch the bus to go shopping downtown, and explored nearby off-campus eateries like Miles Long Sandwich Shop or Neema's favorite takeout chicken joint at the corner of Georgia and Florida Avenues. The greasy chicken wasn't that good, but Neema loved the slogan posted prominently on the wall behind the cashier: "A Chicken Ain't Nothing but a Bird, but the Wings the Thang."

Neema, Faye, and Rose spent a lot of time gossiping about the latest happenings on campus, listening to music, and complaining about classes and dorm life. Connie, the music major down the hall practiced her vocals late at night and often talked to herself. Alice monopolized the one public telephone on the floor, seemingly unaware of the line of women waiting to use it. And, since they'd never seen her in the laundry room, they giddily wondered if Cynthia ever washed her clothes!

The trio also had serious discussions. Neema had received a subscription to *Newsweek* magazine as a high school graduation gift, and Faye had a subscription to *Jet*. The two magazines covered white and Black news and were perfect complements to a liberal arts education. The friends discussed and debated prominent figures and current events, especially the escalating war in Vietnam. Sadly, every student on the floor in their dorm knew someone who had been drafted into the war. *Jet* proudly chronicled the Civil Rights Movement and particularly the work of Martin Luther King, Jr. and Malcolm X. Of course, the girls also had a bit of fun critiquing the Beauty of the Week and catching up on celebrity weddings.

On Friday and Saturday nights, impromptu parties happened in the small dorm rooms in every building in the Quad. Faye and Rose called their room The 308 Club. Neema had a portable record player and stacks of 45s and albums. Rose had a prohibited electric popcorn popper that was a hit. At their weekend parties the trio sang along with music from Motown, practiced their dance moves, drank Coca-Cola, and gobbled up popcorn.

The 308 Club almost turned into a disaster one night when Diana, someone the trio didn't know very well, invited herself into the room. She was from Detroit and a loner. In fact, Neema, Faye, and Rose thought she was kind of weird.

"Hey, ladies," Diana shouted as she entered unexpectedly, "Let's party hardy in here!"

The three friends, products of Christian homes and good home training, didn't know how to get rid of her.

"And I didn't show up empty-handed," she continued. "Look what I got!" Diana opened her purse and pulled out an unopened pint of Bacardi rum. "Want some rum in that Coke?"

None of the trio – just six weeks from leaving home and legally underage – had ever tasted hard liquor. Speechless, they just looked at each other until Faye spoke up.

"Just a little bit," she said timidly. "I want to know what it tastes like."

The three friends sipped politely from their plastic cups of rum and Coke but were not impressed. Neema rendered the group's verdict. "Diana, this is nasty."

Diana, on the other hand, who was steadily refilling her cup, becoming sillier and sillier by the minute. At one point, she realized she was nodding off and pulled a packet of NoDoz pills from her purse. "Have to finish studying tonight for my exam," she explained as she washed down several pills with her rum and Coke. Instead of leaving to go study, Diana stayed and finished the pint of rum. At first, she wouldn't stop laughing, but then she started to hallucinate and cry.

"I'm scared," she wailed. "The room's moving 'round and 'round. I want to go home."

The panic-stricken trio stared at each other.

"What are we going to do?" Faye asked. "Maybe," she suggested, "we should just take her back to her room and let her roommates deal with it."

Neema, Rose, and Faye struggled to keep Diana upright as they walked her to her room, but when they got there, no one was in the room.

Rose worried that if they left her alone, she might die. "And we might go to jail as accessories to a crime, or at the least be expelled from school!"

Neema had another plan. "Let's take her to the Emergency Room at Freedman's Hospital. It's just three blocks away. And we need to go *now*, while she can still walk on her own!" She ran to the desk in the room and typed a quick note. "Let's go!"

They escorted Diana through the Quad lobby, one person on each side and one in back to catch her if she started to stumble. Before they entered the Emergency Room, Neema took out the note she had typed and pinned it on Diana's dress along with her Howard ID. The note said: *My name is Diana Caldwell. I live in 315 Truth Hall. I accidentally took NoDoz while consuming rum. I do not feel well.*

As usual for a weekend, the Emergency Room was packed, so no one noticed when the trio sat Diana in a chair with the note on her dress and the straps of her shoulder bag draped around her neck. They slowly walked out of the hospital and then bolted up the hill to the Quad.

Neither Neema, Faye, nor Rose slept well that night, and they were relieved to see Diana alive the next day. They vowed to never tell anyone what had happened, but that story remained the trio's favorite and funniest about life in the dorm at Howard University.

* * * * *

Despite the highs and lows of dormitory life, Neema was still convinced that she had made the right decision to attend Howard University. The Capstone, as it was sometimes called, was not just a larger version of Fisk, it was a better version, living up to its reputation as the home of the Black race's intellectual elite and training ground for future leaders. Students were taught by African American professors who were noted in their fields and who pushed their budding scholars to challenge traditional paradigms of knowledge and create new ones.

A different but equally influential education took place outside the classroom. Although Howard had its share of rules and curfews, particularly for women living in the dorms, it was not a puritanical church school like Fisk, with strict dress codes and required chapel attendance. The campus had been quiet during the week of freshmen orientation, but it was a different scene the first Friday after the upperclassmen returned to campus. The Yard, as the green lawn in front of Founders Library was known, was filled with people and rowdy laughter. Neema soon discovered that what she had thought of as a tranquil outdoor space was the place that actually defined, more than the campus's classrooms, Howard's school spirit. In fact, it was home to one of the college's most popular events.

Every year on the third Friday in April, new sorority and fraternity recruits, or pledges, would "crossover" to being full members. Neema had witnessed initiation events at Fisk. In fact, her grandmother was a member of a sorority. But the initiations at Howard were especially noteworthy for their over-the-top productions, perhaps because four of the Greek groups had been founded on Howard's campus in the early 1900s. Greeks from nearby universities like Morgan State, Cheyney, and Bowie State attended, proudly sporting their sweaters crowded with the names of their college, their chapter, and the year they pledged. Everyone showed up, from college and Greek alums to the parents of pledges to residents of metro DC. People squeezed into any available spot to see the show. It was a festival of visual and auditory stimulation, and no one left disappointed.

Neema was mesmerized watching her first Greek show on the Yard. The female pledges from Delta Sigma Theta, Alpha Kappa Alpha, and Zeta Phi Beta, and their male counterparts from Omega Psi Phi, Kappa Alpha Psi, and Alpha Phi Alpha converged in The Yard from all directions. Each group had its own tree, fountain, sundial, or other special, designated spot. Neema heard the screams from the crowd and the unique calls of the various fraternities and sororities before she saw the pledges. "O-O-O-OP! Skee-wee!" Lined up by height, the number of pledges could range from ten to thirty.

The pledges of Delta Sigma Theta were called Pyramids. Dressed in crimson and cream, they marched from the Quad to The Yard with their signature duck. The Ivy Club of Alpha Kappa Alpha wore pink blouses and green skirts and carried large, ivy-shaped pillows that matched their outfits. The Kappa men, who had the reputation of being cool and sophisticated, strutted in with their red and white canes. The Alphas, known as intellectuals, headed to their designated spot, the fountain next to Founders Library. As always, the Omega men, affectionately called Que Dogs, stole the show. They didn't march in like the others; they barked and stomped their way into The Yard. Their heads had been shaved, and they wore sunglasses. The lead pledge carried an enormous purple and gold shield and had a dog collar around his neck. The crowd applauded and screamed. Neema and her friends got a kick out of the nicknames being shouted at the pledges by their big sisters and brothers. Obviously, Timex was always late, H-N-I-C (jest for Head Nigger in Charge) was the boss, Two Left Feet surely had no rhythm, and Busy Body was the nosy one.

The Yard was almost a hallowed ground on campus. Throughout the year, and especially in good weather, students started gathering there around noon on Fridays to hang out before, between, and after classes. It was where Howard's diversity was on display and where students could sample the school's many possible social circles as they searched for the right fit for them. It was also where all students could share the same space with other students that they might not otherwise get to know. Undergraduates mingled with graduate students, and DC students who lived at home exchanged information about off-campus parties with dorm students. The somber men in the compulsory ROTC program were an impressive sight as they marched to their practice drills. Some Caribbean students, heads bowed over their dominoes, laughed loudly as they slapped down their tiles on a makeshift table, while others picked up a game of soccer. Greeks would sing their songs. Students who attended the same classes helped each other cram for upcoming exams, and a sprinkling of students would sit alone under trees and read. Best of all, perhaps, was that

The Yard wasn't a conglomerate of highly defined, segregated cliques. Interests and loyalties changed over time, and some students moved in and out of several groups. Neema, Rose, and Faye couldn't wait for Fridays at noon.

One Friday while they were watching one of the sororities sing, Neema was distracted by a loud argument among a large group of international male students. The fast-paced emotional cadence and raised voices caught her attention before she knew what the argument was about. They reminded her of the men she had heard as a child at the baobab tree in Ghana. She stopped and listened to the exchange. It was about who deserved the title of Father of Pan-Africanism – Jomo Kenyatta, Julius Nyerere, Sekou Toure, or Kwame Nkrumah, who one student in the group called weak and cowardly. Before she realized it, she had jumped in to correct what she considered to be some uninformed conclusions about Nkrumah's leadership.

The young man who had criticized Nkrumah frowned at Neema.

"But Jomo Kenyatta knew how to fight colonialism," he argued. "I mean physically fight. His Mau Mau kicked the British asses. Nkrumah was a good orator but not a revolutionary soldier."

"Hold up, brothers!" shouted another. "Sekou Toure is not as well-known as the rest of those guys because Guinea is such a tiny country, but you have to give it to him. His labor unions sent the French running with their tails between their legs. And please don't let me hear the name Julius Nyerere. He just focused on literacy. He was just a schoolmarm who only wanted to teach his people how to read."

Most thought the quip was funny and laughed, but one of the debaters mumbled angrily and walked away.

Neema didn't think that Nkrumah, her father's hero and brother's namesake, was getting a fair hearing and jumped back into the fray.

"I think Nkrumah warrants more consideration," she said. "In 1957, he established the first sub-Saharan independent African country to declare independence. I think that's the kind of action a Father of Pan-Africanism would take. I acknowledge the truths told about the other leaders and their accomplishments, but everything about Nkrumah screams Pan-Africanism. He united the continent by organizing the All Africa People's Conference. Every African leader was welcomed at the table. Not only did he reach out to important actors in the Motherland but, because he had gone to a Black university here in the States and was familiar with Black political activists, he included African American leaders like W.E.B.—"

Neema was rudely interrupted. Noticing her lack of an African or Caribbean accent, someone shouted, "Hey, where you from, sista? You from the States, right? Never been to Africa, and you telling us about something you read in some white folks' books!"

The men looked at her with skepticism, and Neema knew why – women were not supposed to participate in "man talk," especially when the men were from Africa and the Caribbean. But

Neema's mother would go head-to-head with her husband, arguing about politics, current events, or interpretations of books they were reading. Behind her mother's well-mannered, poised Southern persona was a tenacious woman, unafraid to exert her intelligence. Consequently, when Neema saw how the group was dismissing her, she was angry. She turned and walked away as fast as she could.

Neema hadn't gotten far when she heard a male Caribbean voice.

"Wait, wait. How do you know so much about President Nkrumah and Pan-Africanism?"

She turned around and laid eyes on a very gorgeous man.

Nigel Waite III was a sophomore political science major from Kingston, Jamaica. Six-feet tall and lanky, he was moving fast to catch up with her. He had a noticeable rhythmic swagger that exuded poise and confidence. His slightly bowed legs, too long arms, and exact posture were noticeable from a distance, but as he got closer Neema focused on his face. His dark-skinned oval face, thin mustache, full lips, and generous smile prompted Neema to move closer to get a better look. Although the expression *skin as smooth as a baby's butt* is both disgusting and silly, it was the only thought that popped into her mind as she looked at his face. He was smiling, but there was something about him that also signaled "serious brother."

"Sister, you've read a lot about Africa and Pan-Africanism. You were right on it back there. Where were you born and raised?"

"I was born in Accra, Ghana. I can tell by your accent that you weren't born in Africa and probably never been to the Motherland."

"Well actually," he said with a shy grin, "I have. So, let's start over. I think we got off on the wrong foot. I'm Nigel Waite. Got a minute to sit down to talk?"

Neema hesitated for a moment, and then sat down next to Nigel on the steps of Douglass Hall. Although the conversation started a bit awkwardly, it turned into an hour's long light-hearted discussion of their backgrounds and intellectual interests. Neema was pleasantly surprised that Nigel encouraged her to do most of the talking and kept his eyes on her as he listened.

When they were about to part ways, Nigel said, "My friend's having a party tonight. He lives near 14th and Euclid. Why don't you and your friends stop by?"

Neema thought for a moment.

"Nigel, I don't think I can. Besides, we were planning on going to the dance in the Ballroom at the Student Center tonight. Maybe another time." She glanced at her watch and quickly gathered her things. "I better run. I'm about to be late for class."

Neema couldn't wait to tell Rose and Faye about the fine brother from Jamaica she had met. She hurried through the description of the debate and the chauvinistic brothers to get to what she really wanted to share.

"Tall, dark, fine, brilliant, but not full of himself or arrogant. And that accent. I love it!" Neema tried to imitate Nigel's introduction with a Jamaican patois. "Way-t, way-t," he said. "How ya know so much 'bout Nkrumah and Pan-Africanism?" They all laughed at how comical her imitation was.

Rose wanted to know more. "Well, when are you going to see him again?"

"I don't know," Neema said. "He invited us to some off-campus party tonight, but I told him we were going to the Ballroom."

"What?" Rose was dumbfounded. "You mean to tell me you passed up an opportunity to hang out with a fine brother in order to go to that stupid Ballroom dance? You must have lost your damn mind!"

The Ballroom dance on Friday nights was the only game in town for freshmen, and no self-respecting sophomore would be caught dead there. Yet, Nigel found himself standing, almost hiding, really, behind a column in the cavernous room where one wall had floor-to-ceiling windows overlooking the McMillan Reservoir. He had no intention of staying; he just wanted to see Neema's face before heading to his off-campus party. She was easy to spot.

Neema was dancing with a Howard "block boy" from DC and had mastered the intricate hand dance in the two months she had been on campus. She moved so smoothly that other DC students kept breaking in to dance with her. She had barely sat down on the sofa with Rose and Faye when another guy swooped her up. Nigel watched as she effortlessly did the Philly Dog and Philly Cha Cha, two of the newest dance crazes. Neema never missed a beat.

While returning to her spot on the sofa, Neema caught a glimpse of Nigel leaning nonchalantly against one of the columns.

"Ok," she said out the side of her mouth to her friends, "he's here."

"Who's here?" asked Faye.

"Nigel. Don't look! Don't look! Listen up. If he comes over here, pretend that you don't know anything about him. Rose, when I introduce him, why don't you say something like, 'Sorry, I didn't get that. What's your name again?' *Do not* chat him up or ask him any questions. I don't want him to think I'm excited to see him."

Nigel slowly worked his way through the crowd toward Neema.

"Hey, Nigel, what are you doing here?" Neema introduced Rose and Faye. "I thought you were going to another party."

"Oh, yeah, uh, I'm, um, I'm waiting on my ride," he said, trying to sound convincing. "Wow, where'd you learn to dance like that?"

"Africa," she answered, hoping she was piquing his interest.

Neema invited him to join them, and Nigel sat with the Truth Hall trio as they chattered and giggled. When the DJ played a slow song, Smokey Robinson and the Miracles' *You Really Got a Hold on Me*, Nigel grabbed Neema's hand and walked her to the dance floor.

Neema appreciated that Nigel didn't try to pull her too close, but when he started talking about Nkrumah while Smokey crooned in the background, she was confused. Why, she wondered, would he skip his party, come to a freshman event, wait for a slow song to dance with me, just to pontificate about African politics? After the three-minute song ended, Nigel said goodnight and left as quickly as he had appeared.

* * * * *

October 1966 was Neema's first Homecoming, and the Black Power activists on campus had nominated a student with an Afro hairstyle for Homecoming Queen. Although a lot of Howard students had Afros, the hairstyle was still controversial. Delta Sigma Theta and Alpha Kappa Alpha had nominees with more traditional looks. The coronation was in Cramton Auditorium, and everyone on campus was excited about who would win. Neema and her buddies were rooting for the Black Nationalist sister with the Afro.

When the curtain opened to reveal the winner, the auditorium rang with a deafening roar that could be heard across the street in the men's dorm. They were witnessing history. The new Homecoming Queen was a beautiful young woman with natural hair that fittingly resembled a crown. She was a member of SNCC, the Student Nonviolent Coordinating Committee, and she and her nationalist colleagues were redefining the Civil Rights Movement and what it meant to attend a historically Black college.

Neema was inspired and decided she wanted to style her thick wavy hair into an Afro. And she knew exactly who she wanted to look like. While doing research for her political science honors paper on the Marxist professor Herbert Marcuse, Neema had seen a picture of the professor and his Ph.D. student, Angela Davis. Neema checked the book out of the library, rounded up her Truth Hall crew of girlfriends, and showed them the picture.

"What do you think?" she asked them.

Everyone agreed that Angela Davis's Afro would be perfect for Neema, and the team went to work. Everyone contributed some type of hair product – shampoo, conditioner, moisturizer, gel, holding spray – and there were lots of "Sheens" on the table – Afro Sheen, Ultra Sheen, Soft Sheen. Someone had a big Afro pick with a wood handle carved in the shape of a Black Power fist. Faye used it to gently comb out Neema's hair. When it was time to begin cutting, everyone had an opinion.

"You're cutting too much off the top. Look at the picture of Angela Davis. It's even on all sides!"

"The back's too long. Cut off a little more."

Three hours later, the Truth Hall gang declared the project a success. They agreed that they had transformed Neema's hair into one of the largest and most stunning Afros on Howard's campus.

Neema was delighted and had one more beauty procedure in mind – pierced ears. Not only did the Afro-wearing sisters on campus have head-turning Afros, but they also wore amazing earrings. Usually handmade, the earring designs were unique and drop-dead gorgeous – large hoops with beads, tassels that draped the neck, shapes like the continent of Africa, and so many others. And not one pair was made for non-pierced ears.

She and Rose learned that a student in Wheatley Hall named Marsha was very good at piercing ears. More importantly, she charged only five dollars. Rose lost the coin flip, so she was first in the chair.

Marsha lined up her surgical tools – a cup of ice from the cafeteria, a long sewing needle, a bottle of alcohol, cotton balls, a discarded cork from a wine bottle, and Rose's and Neema's new stud earrings.

Marsha used the alcohol and cotton balls to sanitize the needle and the earrings. Next, she numbed Rose's ear lobes with ice. Rose closed her eyes as Marsha placed the cork behind her right ear lobe and pushed the needle through the front.

"Ouch!" Rose screamed.

Neema watched in dismay as Marsha then pierced Rose's left ear lobe and witnessed another shout of pain from Rose. She was ready to run, but Rose wasn't having it.

"On, no, you don't," she said, choking back a tear, "You're staying! We agreed to do this together."

Neema sat in the chair. Suddenly a picture of a keloid scar popped in her head. In her enthusiasm for the new Black revolutionary look, Neema hadn't thought about the large puffy scars Black people often get after a cut in their skin. Too late to turn back now, she thought.

For the rest of her life, every time she put on a pair of earrings from her vast collection, she would look at her left lobe that had been punctured at an angle and her right lobe, where the puncture was higher than on the left, and chuckled about her mutilation by a well-meaning student in Wheatley Hall.

When Nigel first saw her Afro and pierced ears, he seemed very pleased. However, Neema couldn't exactly determine to what extent he was pleased. His milquetoast compliment was underwhelming.

"Look at the sister! Straight from Mother Africa. You got it going on."

Neema's hairstyle and earrings were not the only transformation. She looked at herself in the mirror and saw a different woman – more confident, prouder, and more convinced that accepting the college administration's conservative, outdated mentality was not an option.

Neema and Nigel continued to run into each other in The Yard. Nigel was the ultimate Yard crosser, at home with Africans, Caribbean people, flirtatious sorority women, sophisticated New Yorkers, and reserved small-town Southerners. He was a backslapper, a hand-shaker, and a hugger who, as they say, never met a stranger and remembered the names of everyone he met. He was a natural politician. In fact, few students knew but he was the grandson of a former Jamaican Governor-General and the son of a current member of Jamaica's Upper House. He jokingly referred to himself as a "poor Jamaican boy trying to make his way in this world," but that was far from the truth.

Over time, Neema and Nigel became good friends. They were avid readers and liked to argue about politics and history. They always met at Founders Library, where they studied for exams and wrote papers. When Neema was late, Nigel would wait for her on the library steps so they could find seats together. He never complained. When it was time to begin registering for second semester classes, Nigel asked Neema to consider joining him as a political science major. She agreed. Even though he was a year ahead of her, they took a few of the same classes together. When Neema couldn't find a book she needed to complete her Honors English term paper, Nigel took her on the Metro bus to the Library of Congress. On the complete opposite of the cultural spectrum, he surprised her with a trip to the off-campus Howard Theater to see James Brown and Otis Redding. Neema didn't know exactly what to call these outings. They were definitely not dates. He never even tried to kiss her. Neema tried not to be disappointed.

The Punch Out in the Student Center was not Neema's favorite place, but on this particular day, she was desperate to find something to eat before her next class. The windowless junk food haven on the building's bottom level greeted students with smells of greasy French fries and onions. And, yes, there was a bottle of hot sauce on every table. Everyone had a good time at the Punch Out. Unfortunately, some students spent too much time there playing Bid Whist and Gin Rummy. For a lot of those students, the name Punch Out predicted their likely outcome. You didn't see them the following semester.

As Neema turned to leave, she was surprised to spot Nigel in a corner, grinning and rubbing the back of one of his Jamaican homegirls. She was whispering in his ear and laughing. Neema couldn't hear the conversation but knew for sure that they were *not* discussing Pan-Africanism. Once outside, Neema gave herself a "get a grip" talk. Nigel, she reminded herself, is just a friend. Evidently, he just likes your superior mind and Pan-African consciousness, not your smile, eyes, or shape. You're his intellectual comrade and will probably never be his lover.

The end of Neema's first year at Howard was two weeks away. Nigel was going home to Jamaica, and she was headed to Nashville. Still a bit unnerved by seeing him in the Punch Out, she avoided the usual places where she might run into him and declined his offer to study together for finals. The day before she was to catch a train home, Nigel buzzed her from the lobby of Tubman Quad and asked her to come downstairs.

"Hi, stranger," he said, "what's the problem? I'm leaving in three days, and your roommate said you are leaving tomorrow. Were you gonna leave without saying goodbye to me?"

"Of course not, Nigel," she lied. "I've just been busy packing to go home. I'm really excited about the summer. I have a good job and plan to take a couple of trips to Atlanta to hang out with my homeboy at Morehouse."

"Well, sounds like fun. Didn't know you had a good friend at Morehouse. Well, have a great summer. Let's definitely check in with each other in September."

Neema kept her distance, and Nigel had to lean forward give her an awkward hug and pat on the back.

The next day Neema boarded the train at Union Station. She had a lot to think about. The truth was that she was dreading her summer job and didn't have plans to visit any male friend anywhere. Most of all, she was disappointed that her relationship with Nigel wasn't romantic.

When Neema exited the train station in Nashville, Lily took one look at her daughter's Afro, pierced ears, and large hoop earrings and launched into her signature "mad as hell" performance. Lily didn't "show-out," a term she reserved for the behavior of "low class" Black folks. Rather, she narrowed her eyes to stare at her victim and spoke in a low voice through clenched teeth, enunciating each syllable as if she were talking to a deaf person who needed to read her lips.

"Neema Washington, why are you embarrassing me?" As always, Lily thought everything was about her. "You look hideous. Your beautiful hair is gone! You have holes in your ears and earrings hanging on your shoulders. Who did this to you? Joseph," she turned to her husband, "is *this* what they're teaching our daughter at Howard University?"

"None of the young women around here look this way," her mother was saying. "No one! Now take off those ridiculous earrings and get over to Miss Ella Mae's salon so she can fix your hair!"

"I like this look, Mother, and my hair doesn't need fixing. It's not broken. You'll like it more over time. Trust me."

Later that night, Neema went into her father's office for one of their special talks.

"Love your hair, Baby Girl, but not sure about those earrings. Maybe you can tone it down a bit," he suggested.

Neema reluctantly took off her earrings.

"Whatever way you style your hair, you are a beautiful African queen. You will always be my Nefertiti, the Egyptian goddess whose name means a beautiful woman has come."

Neema hugged her father and then they talked for hours about Howard and her new friends. She hadn't realized how much she had missed her dad and his calming presence.

After the excitement of her freshman year at Howard, the summer break felt long and boring, and the constant flashbacks she had of good times with Nigel only left her sad. Her dull summer job added to her misery. Neema had been hired as a "floating" secretary at Fisk, a person who substituted for vacationing staff. Week after week, she moved from office to office on a mostly vacant campus and operated the main switchboard, answered phones, took messages, typed memos, and, mostly, stared at the clock. At least twice a week, one of Lily's colleagues would stop by to say hello, but they were really coming to see her big Afro, which caused quite a stir at the conservative school. The Fisk ladies' comments were all some variation on the theme, *what happened to your beautiful hair?* The summer of 1967 was a nightmare.

* * * * *

At the beginning of September, Neema returned to Howard for her second year. On the train ride to DC, Neema thought about the fact that Nigel hadn't written to her all summer, but then she hadn't written to him either. She wondered what their relationship would be like this year. They would have political science classes together, and they were both officers of the Du Bois Political Science Club, so it was just a matter of time before they would come face-to-face.

The day of reckoning came a few days after she arrived on campus. She was headed for the gym to register for classes when Nigel's voice startled her and she almost tripped on the uneven sidewalk. Nigel was sitting on the steps of Founders Library.

"Neema, Neema!" he called. "I was waiting for you. It's registration day and I thought we'd register together like we did last spring."

"Really?" Neema asked nonchalantly as she continued to walk.

"Hey, wait up!" He took a few quick steps to catch up with her. "What's going on?"

"What's going on?" Neema was incredulous. "I don't hear from you all summer and now you act like we've got standing dates?"

"Okay," Nigel said good-naturedly, "fair enough, but hear me out. I really missed you."

Neema stopped walking and looked at him skeptically.

"Really," he said, "the summer was unbearable thinking about you. I've never met a sister like you. Of course, you're a beautiful woman. How could any man not notice? But you threw me off guard because you're also brilliant. Your mind, not your beauty, defines you. I just didn't know how to approach you. Every move I planned just didn't feel right – too aggressive, too suggestive, or too silly."

Neema smiled as she thought back to their strange evening at the Ballroom dance.

"I thought with you in Nashville and me in Jamaica, I could put some distance between us and clear my head, but it didn't work. Neema, I want to spend more time with you. I want to be with you. I need to be with you."

Neema was blown away and tried to be cool, but she was thrilled.

Neema and Nigel became constant companions, together on campus during the week and in his newly acquired apartment near Howard on weekends. Nigel and his Jamaican roommate invited friends to visit, and Neema enjoyed the impromptu parties and spirited political debates. She especially looked forward to spending time with Nigel in the privacy of his bedroom, where they would lay together talking softly and snuggling, or kissing passionately, or just holding each other quietly. She felt safe in his arms. Neema was a virgin and had told Nigel that she was afraid to have sex, especially since she didn't know much about birth control. He assured her that he understood and never tried to remove her clothing or coax her to do anything she wasn't ready to. But Neema knew that it wouldn't be long before she and Nigel would make love, so she and Rose searched through the DC phone book looking for a women's health center located near a bus line they knew. They found one, and Rose accompanied Neema to what turned out to be an uneventful doctor's visit. She left with a prescription for birth control pills, but getting the prescription filled created another stressful moment. In her paranoia, Neema was worried that she would run into someone from Howard at the pharmacy and that they would know what she was getting. She eventually went to a People's Drug Store far away from campus.

Neema couldn't figure out a way to inform Nigel that she was taking the pill. Every scenario she came up with seemed contrived and a bit sluttish. So Neema took the pills and decided the right time would reveal itself.

One afternoon, Nigel told Neema that he had to run back to his apartment because he had forgotten the flyers for that night's student government meeting. She volunteered to walk the five blocks with him. When they arrived at Nigel's building, he went in while Neema waited outside. Nigel's roommate rarely went to class, and she didn't like to go in the apartment when he might be entertaining some woman or holding court with his Jamaican buddies. Neema was surprised when Nigel quickly returned and told her she could come in because his roommate was out.

Neema and Nigel made tuna sandwiches and listened to Aretha's newest record, *You Make Me Feel Like a Natural Woman.* Nigel grabbed Neema's hand and pulled her out of the chair. "Let's dance."

They held each other close and danced slowly, their bodies moving as Aretha soulfully declared that she was indeed a woman. Aretha's words echoed in Neema's head and they ended up in Nigel's bedroom. When Neema started to undress, Nigel was both shocked and excited.

"Neema, are you sure you want to do this?"

The intensity of her kiss gave him her answer.

Later, when Nigel walked Neema to the dorm and hugged her goodbye, he whispered in her ear, "I love you, Neema Washington."

It took Neema a week to tell Rose and Faye that she and Nigel had had sex. After the initial shock, both friends, who were virgins, wanted to know all the details. Faye, who was in a serious relationship and spending more time away from Truth Hall, was particularly curious.

"What made you decide the time was right? What did it feel like? Did it hurt?"

Neema took a minute to respond. "I don't know, really. It just happened. I was scared and nervous, but I also really wanted it to happen. I think you just know."

Neema and Nigel were now inseparable. He was her friend and lover, always gentle and never demanding. He was her intellectual equal, never condescending or chauvinistic. He was her sounding board, never interrupting her train of thought. He was her comforter, wiping her tears when life disappointed. And he was a dreamer who encouraged her to dream along with him.

* * * * *

Discontent among Howard University students had been percolating long before Neema arrived on campus, but it boiled over on March 17, 1968. Nigel caught up with Neema just as she was about to enter her class.

"Neema, come with me," he said as he grabbed her hand. "Things are getting ready to jump off in Cramton Auditorium. Without consulting the Student Government, President Nesbitt and Dean Stovall invited General Hershey, the Director of the Selective Service, to speak at an assembly. Can you believe that! Brothers are being drafted and killed in Vietnam while white boys get a free pass. Not to mention Howard having some bull shit compulsory ROTC." Nigel was fired up. "Muhammad Ali is right. 'I ain't got no quarrel with them Vietcong.' Black folks just tryin' to survive racism in America!"

Neema cheered as a group of brothers stormed the stage and escorted the general out of the building. One demonstrator held up a sign, *Vietnam, Hell No!* This was a defining moment at Howard. The students were making it clear that they weren't interested in integrating into a white world. They were focused on self-determination and the development of Black political and cultural institutions. Black consciousness had exploded.

Two days later, at the urging of campus leaders, students rushed to the front of the administration building in response to Dean Stovall's announcement that he wanted Howard to become the "Black Harvard." Students were livid. One student speaker yelled, "Hell no! Harvard better think about becoming the White Howard." The students rejected the administration's "plantation mentality" and insisted on a curriculum centered on African American nationalism and liberation. In a moment of spontaneity, students marched inside the building and occupied it for five days. Protestors taped a huge handwritten sign over the front doors of the building: *Closed.* Another sign boldly proclaimed that Howard was no longer named after Union General Oliver Otis Howard. From now on it would simply be called The Black University. Inside the building, students went to work setting up committees and pledged to stay until their demands were met.

The Food Committee accepted donations from nearby businesses. The medical and nursing students operated a 24-hour first aid station. Students in the College of Engineering and Architecture designed an elaborate public address system. A security force discussed how to respond and ensure everyone's safety if the DC Police showed up. Neema, remembering the skills she had learned during her summer job at Fisk, volunteered to operate the university switchboard and taught Rose and Faye how to operate the complicated circuit board of jacks, wires, and cords. They were inundated with calls from supporters around the country who were anxious to help. The Sanitation Committee had a major challenge keeping the five-story building clean. The Hospitality Committee screened requests from groups like the Trinidadian steel pan musicians, African drummers and dancers, and jazz soloists and musicians from the College of Fine Arts who wanted to provide entertainment to the stressed-out students. The whole committee system worked more efficiently than the university's convoluted registration process. One elated student hoisted a sign that provided much needed comic relief: *Who Said Niggers Can't Organize?*

Students took turns in the evening going to their dorms to bathe and change clothes. At bedtime, weary students took up every inch of space on the floors to sleep, even if just briefly. Finally, on March 23, 1968, the student leaders, Board of Trustees, and the university president agreed to negotiate. The administration agreed that there would be changes to the curriculum and more student input and control over budgets, guest speakers, and the student newspaper. No charges would be filed against the protestors, and students wouldn't be penalized for classes and assignments that were missed during the occupation. The only things that the students didn't get were the resignations of the president and dean.

When the announcement was made, a thunderous roar shook the administration building. Joyful but exhausted students filed out carrying their blankets, pillows, and books. Resolved to never surrender to "The Man" or abandon The Black Power Movement, they danced on the sidewalks as the public address system blasted The Impressions' song, *We're a Winner*.

The joy was short-lived. Just eleven days after the student's victory, Nigel ran from his apartment to Neema's dorm. As soon as she saw her disheveled, breathless soul mate, she knew something was terribly wrong.

"Neema, Martin Luther King is dead! Shot in Memphis after a march for sanitation workers. Oh, Neema, this is so awful!"

Neema cried and thought about the time in 1960 when she was eleven. Dr. Martin Luther King, Jr. was organizing a citywide boycott in Nashville, and her father introduced him at a rally at their church. When Neema was introduced to Dr. King, he had given her a hug.

Later that evening, as Neema and Nigel sat in The Yard with other students lamenting the assassination and railing against America's racism, they suddenly heard the roar of police cars, their sirens blasting, speeding up Georgia Avenue. Within minutes, they could smell smoke. The nation's capital, like other major urban cities, was on fire. In DC, four days of rioting resulted in more than a thousand fires and thirteen million dollars in damages. The National Guard was called in, and Howard closed the campus and directed all students to go home.

* * * * *

Joseph and Lily were frantic about the riots and glad that Neema was coming home. They suggested that she invite Nigel, whom they had never met. Their daughter was obviously in love with the young man and was talking about spending her life with him in Accra or maybe Kingston. Neema made all manner of excuses, but Nigel thought it was a good idea for him to meet her parents.

The visit turned out better than Neema had expected. She could barely pry Nigel out of her father's office. They spent hours discussing African and Caribbean politics and the general condition of Black people in America. Her mother, as expected, was cautious and a bit standoffish but polite. She was not as easily won over by Nigel's natural charm and innate political skills as her husband was. She perked up, however, when he described his childhood trips to London with his grandfather who had been Governor-General. He shared pictures of Kingston, including pictures of his family's scenic beach house in Ocho Rios.

One evening when they were alone in the kitchen, Neema asked, "Mom, what do you think of Nigel?"

Lily continued to wipe down the counter and mumbled what was as close to a compliment as she could muster. "If you like him, I like him."

It was a disappointing answer, but Neema had promised herself that she wouldn't get upset with her mother while Nigel was visiting.

Lily stopped wiping the counter and turned to face her daughter.

"Just don't bring him to church this Sunday. It's way too early to introduce him to our church family and friends. He's your first boyfriend, not your fiancé. As far as I know, he hasn't asked you to marry him or invited you to meet his family. So, let's slow down and see where this is going."

Neema's father, on the other hand, was impressed.

"Neema, that young man is going places. He's smart and is confident about who he is."

"Daddy, I think he's the one," Neema confessed. "Sort of reminds me of you."

"Whoa, Baby Girl, slow down!" he cautioned. "Take your time. Nigel seems like a wonderful guy, but matters of the heart can take unexpected twists and turns. Stay focused on your dreams, and believe me, the right man will find you."

Yes, Father. The right man will find me.

* * * * *

The spring of 1969 was the end of Neema's junior year and Nigel's last year at Howard. It was a bittersweet time for Neema. Nigel was planning to return to Jamaica after graduation to assist in his father's recently announced campaign for Prime

Minister but promised to return to DC after the election. Although Nigel had never mentioned the word "marriage," Neema believed that they were headed in that direction and allowed herself to fantasize about a Christmas wedding in Howard's Rankin Chapel decorated with red and white poinsettias.

Neema tried to share Nigel's excitement about the election but soon realized that she was an outsider. She only had a superficial understanding of the more nuanced aspects of Jamaican culture, history, and politics. This became painfully clear at Nigel's graduation party that his parents held at the Jamaican Embassy in DC. Everyone was polite, but they never developed a conversation with Neema beyond the obligatory questions that required a one-word response: "Where are you from? Are you enjoying yourself? Are you graduating tomorrow? Have you ever been to Jamaica?"

As the hours slowly passed and the liquor flowed freely, Neema found herself sitting alone with a smile pasted on her face. She was bored, lonely, and vaguely insulted. Nigel didn't seem to notice. He and his father were busy glad-handing everyone and sucking the air out of the room. The guests had separated into same-sex groups and were either talking politics and sports or planning manicures and shopping trips. Nigel's mother occasionally peeked at her in much the same way that her mother had kept her eye on Nigel when he was in Nashville. Karma's a bitch, Neema thought. She feigned a headache and asked Nigel to call her a cab.

Over the summer, Nigel frequently sent Neema love letters from Jamaica, but by September they have devolved into brief, infrequent updates about the campaign. When Nigel's father won the election that winter, Neema was happy because it meant that Nigel would soon be returning to DC. When she received a letter from him on February 14, 1970, Valentine's Day, she couldn't wait to open it, hoping it would let her know when he was coming.

Dear Neema,

Writing this letter is the most difficult thing I have ever had to do. I have thrown away many drafts trying to find the right words with the right tone. Still, this letter is a poor excuse for my numerous attempts.

Neema immediately thought about that registration day when he had said something similar before telling her how much he wanted to be with her. She smiled as she kept reading.

I love you and would never hurt you. I didn't believe in love at first sight and resisted the idea. But the first time I saw you in The Yard, going head-to-head with the brothers about Nkrumah, I was hooked.

She, too, had been smitten with him that day.

Right now, my life is in constant turmoil and uncertainty.

This surprised her. He hadn't hinted that anything was wrong in any of his earlier communications. She frowned. The letter continued.

I've re-connected with a woman I have known since my childhood, Edith Merriweather. She is the sister of my friend, Trevor. I never paid much attention to her since she is four years older than I am. Three years ago, she returned home after finishing her Master's degree in Finance at the London School of Economics. She ran and won a seat in Parliament, and the Prime Minister appointed her Minister of Finance.

Neema wondered where this was going. She had been standing, but now she sat down.

Edith and I worked very closely on Dad's campaign and spent lots of time together. Neema, I am 1400 miles away from you, but the gossip mill in Kingston works amazingly well. I would never want you to hear about Edith from anyone but me. Neema, I need time to think things through and find out if we are meant to be lifetime partners.

Neema was stunned. Was he saying that he and this Edith person were thinking about getting married? The bastard! She was really pissed at his pathetic ending.

I will always love you, Nigel

So that was it. Over, just like that. Ending as unceremoniously as it had begun. Neema's dream of living happily ever after with the only man she had loved had turned into a nightmare. She felt angry, sad, and foolish. She stopped going to classes. She slept all day and cried all night. Rose and Faye tried to comfort her, but Neema refused all their efforts to help. Faye took her meal card and brought food to her room, but she wouldn't eat. She tried to get Neema to contact her classmates for their lecture notes, but she wouldn't. Rose, as usual, was more pragmatic.

"Hell with the nigger! You can find another man, a smarter and better-looking one. I knew there was something about him that I didn't like, but I couldn't put my finger on it. Trust me; you're better off without him!"

Neema tried to figure out why her relationship with Nigel had fallen apart. First, she blamed her parents. Their relationship had always been a mystery to her. They hadn't been a good model for her. Then she blamed herself for not having dated anyone in high school or college before Nigel. What kind of dummy, she thought, falls in love with the first guy she saw on campus during the first half of the first semester? Then she landed on the one person who she decided deserved all the blame – Nigel.

That son of a bitch, she fumed to herself. He played me like a fiddle. Took advantage of the fact that I was a virgin and never had another boyfriend. He strung me along for three years. Because of him, I missed all my opportunities to meet other guys.

Coward! He knew he was never coming back to the States. Knew he'd never have to face me again. I hate him! Hate him, hate him, hate him!

But deep down, she knew that she still loved him.

Spring break was in a week, and Neema shamelessly invited herself to Rose's home in Hampton, Virginia. She was definitely *not* going to Nashville and subject herself to her mother's *I told you so.*

The trip was a nice getaway for Neema. She had interacted with Rose's parents on campus several times and liked them a lot. Rose had told her lots of stories about her older sisters and baby niece, and she was looking forward to meeting them. Everyone gathered at Rose's parents' house for Easter, which fell on the last Sunday of Neema's spring break. Watching Rose's big family interact, Neema couldn't help but envy how they all seemed to enjoy each other's company. There was lots of laughter around the dining room table, and everyone had fun watching sports on TV after dinner.

Rose took Neema on a tour of Hampton Institute, where her father worked in Student Affairs. There were no students around because of spring break, so Rose and Neema walked around the beautiful campus laughing about Truth Hall drama and contemplating their future. Rose had been accepted to Harvard's Law School and was headed to Boston. Faye was engaged and planned to accept a high school teaching position in Savannah, her hometown.

"Neema," Rose said, "come to Boston with me. I don't have a roommate yet, so you can stay with me until you figure out what you want to do. Maybe you can look around Harvard and see if you like any of the graduate programs. I know you could get a fellowship."

Neema thanked Rose but declined. "You've been there for me since the day we met four years ago, but I don't think what I want is in Boston."

After spring break, Neema tried to come up with a plan for the rest of her life. It was six weeks before graduation, and she was clueless about her future. She was graduating summa cum laude, and her proud parents would be expecting to hear what their daughter planned to do next when they arrived for the commencement. Otherwise, she would end up back in her parents' house.

As Neema entered historic Douglass Hall, she noticed a group of young white people sitting at tables in the foyer. Two huge signs hung on the walls behind them: *One Person Can Make a Difference, and Everyone Should Try* and *Now That You Have a Degree, Get an Education. Join the Peace Corps.*

Neema studied the signs like a foreigner with limited English skills, reading and re-reading the words in her heads. Suddenly, she broke into a huge smile. Forget about making a difference and getting an education, she thought. I'm going back to the one place where I feel at home. Without so much as picking up a brochure, Neema approached the older woman who seemed to be in charge. She had only one question: "Do you place volunteers in Accra, Ghana?"

"Indeed, we do," said the woman, and she launched into her well-rehearsed recruitment speech.

Neema interrupted, "Yes, I know a little bit about the place."

The lady seemed slightly amused.

"You'll find Ghana to be more splendid and complex than the descriptions in your books here at Howard. But no worries. We have excellent orientations and classes to bring everybody up to speed."

Neema tried not to roll her eyes.

Rose thought the Peace Corps idea was misguided and actively discouraged Neema.

"Why are you doing this Neema? Don't answer because I know why – to get over that pompous Negro. Neema, that man has moved on, and you should to. But not to Ghana, for goodness' sake!"

"Of all people," Neema said, "I thought you'd understand!"

Undeterred, Neema signed up for the Peace Corps' Get Acquainted reception at DC's main library and left with an application. Sooner than she had expected, she was accepted. In a rehearsed and hyped-up delivery, she shared the news with her parents on graduation day.

"Sit down. I've got a surprise for you."

Joseph and Lily quickly glanced at each other and then sat down on two metal folding chairs.

"Guess what?" Neema said cheerfully, "I joined the Peace Corp! And you won't believe where I have been assigned. Accra!"

Both her parents were stunned and speechless. Not wanting to give them a chance to object, Neema rushed on.

"I'm *so* excited! This is my chance to help make some positive changes in my birth home just like the two of you did. And you know the first thing I'm going to do? I'm gonna find Aunt Eni and walk along Labadi Beach and stroll around Makola Market. I can't wait!"

"So, you and Nigel are going to Accra," Lily asked skeptically.

"No, Mother, Nigel and I broke up."

"So, Nigel walked out on you, and now you're going to Accra? You've got to be joking. Please, Neema, please don't do this. You really don't know anything about Accra. You were too young to remember. You're just running away from Nigel."

Neema didn't respond to her mother's typically negative reaction. She was counting on her father to be excited that she was pursuing her dream. He wasn't. Joseph looked down at his hands. They were clasped together like those of a man pleading for mercy.

"I, I don't know," he stuttered. "You sure about this? Why don't you hold up on this for a while, and let's think it through? I thought you had always planned to go to graduate school. Come home, take a break, and we can figure out your next step together."

Neema was disappointed. "Daddy, I'm taking your advice. Remember? 'Follow your dreams.'"

"Good luck with finding them in Accra, Neema Washington!" Lily interjected. "Why do you always have to learn the hard way?"

Lily Washington had always been an enigma to Neema. Clearly, Lily was a smart woman. Neema figured that, because her mother had been born in 1922, she would have had to negotiate an unimaginable series of obstacles created by racism and sexism. How, Neema wondered, had she survived all those hurdles? Maybe those difficult formative years explain why she seems angry all the time. But Neema didn't know much about her mother's personal life, so it was hard to come up with answers. Sometimes Lily seemed to enjoy reminiscing about her childhood in Little Rock, how she met Joseph at Fisk, and their early years together in Africa. Even then, though, her mother's emotions could zigzag from laughing out loud with joy and pride to holding back tears from embarrassment and anger.

Sadly, Neema couldn't figure out how her parents had fallen in love. They seemed so different in values, social class, experiences, and personality. She was the storm, and he was the calm at the center. Maybe some guy at Fisk had broken Lily's heart, and Joseph had been her fallback guy. The more Neema tried to connect the scattered puzzle pieces of her mother's life, the more questions she had.

CHAPTER TWO

LITTLE ROCK, ARKANSAS
POPE CITY, GEORGIA

June 7 was a picture-perfect summer morning. Lily Robinson tried on her new outfit – white suit, white silk blouse adorned with a white lace collar, wrist-length white cotton gloves, and white heels. She perched the borrowed white pillbox hat on her head and draped its long net veil over her face and under her chin. She smiled as she stared at herself in the full-length mirror nailed behind the door of her dorm room. She had tried on this outfit at least once a day for the past week, and each time she loved what she saw. With a week-old Bachelor of Arts degree in Music Education, Lily was just twenty-four hours away from marrying her college sweetheart, Joseph Washington.

Lily met Joseph at Fisk University in 1939, where they were members of the famed Fisk Jubilee Singers. Lily first took a good look at Joseph during her sophomore year when the choir director startled both her and Joseph by asking them to step forward and audition for solo parts of the Negro spiritual, *Steal Away.*

The choir director insisted on "whitewashing" Negro spirituals.

"This is Fisk University, not a cotton field," he often shouted to his students. "The word is Lo-o-or-d, not Lawd. And it's not 'ain't got long to stay here.' The grammatically correct line is 'I don't have long to stay here.'"

The choir director's operatic versions of "slave" songs required phrasing, timing, and articulation. Any emotional non-verbal expressions like handclapping or swaying, or verbal affirmations like "Amen" resulted in a failing grade in his Choral Performance class.

People tended not to notice Joseph. He kind of blended in – just another tenor, another guy who didn't play sports and wasn't in a fraternity, one of those nice, dark-skinned guys who didn't attract a lot of attention. But on that day at choir practice, when Joseph Washington belted out *Steal Away,* he was invisible no more. Despite the restrictive instructions of the choir director, Joseph's voice could not be constrained. It carried with it the ethos and memories of enslaved ancestors. Lily had sung this spiritual hundreds of times but with little passion. This was the first time she had visualized people running for freedom through swamps, hunted by barking dogs. After Joseph sang, Lily stepped forward for her audition and found herself singing as she had never sung before. Joseph Washington and Lily Robinson not only became a duet in the Jubilee Singers, but they also became lovers.

Well, lovers would be an exaggeration of their relationship. With Fisk's unyielding restrictions and curfews, Lily and Joseph mainly ate lunch and dinner together in the cafeteria and worshipped together at mandatory chapel services. Women could "receive company" in the lobby of their dorms, where they sat and talked. They were chaperoned at dances in the Student Center and during the ten-year-old movies that were shown in the gymnasium. If they managed to steal a tender touch or brief kiss, they considered themselves lucky. Going off-campus had to be pre-arranged, and women were not permitted to leave campus alone. Nashville was strictly segregated and a dangerous place for all Black students. Despite this restrictive environment, Lily and Joseph's affection for each other grew, and they knew that they wanted to be with each other for the rest of their lives. Neither dated anyone else during their four years on campus.

Lily was dressed three hours before her wedding ceremony. She paced around the tiny dorm room, occasionally peering out at the parking lot to see if her parents had arrived yet from Little Rock, and then back again to gaze at her image in the mirror. A loud knock startled her.

"Lily," one of the resident assistants said, "your parents are in the lobby waiting for you."

* * * * *

Shirley Robinson had started planning her daughter's wedding practically since the day Lily was born. The celebration she was throwing for Lily's sixteenth birthday was almost as elaborate as the one she envisioned for her wedding someday.

"Wake up, Lily darling!" she chirped as she burst into Lily's bedroom. "This evening is your Sweet Sixteen party, and we've got a lot to do. I'm going to the church to make sure the ushers decorate Fellowship Hall exactly as I instructed. The Funeral Repast Committee needs to start on the food preparation and table set-ups right away. Your father will drop you off at the beauty parlor for your final touch-up. Goodness! I still need to hear your welcome remarks. And please remember to smile. Oh, one more thing. I have something very important to show you. I'll be right back." And she rushed out as briskly as she had arrived.

Lily lay in bed, dreading her mother's return. Like everything in her life, she had no control over how she would spend her birthday. She didn't even want this party! The guests were the children of her mother's sorority sisters, not her friends. Now her mother was about to spring something else on her. She knew that she'd just have to go along with whatever it was, so she tried not to focus on how miserable and angry she felt.

Shirley returned to Lily's room with a red and blue floral hatbox tied with gold-colored ropes. Excitedly, she opened the box and carefully peeled back layers of tissue paper.

"As you know, Lily," she began, "W.E.B. Du Bois taught at Fisk when your father and I were students there. When his daughter, Yolande, married the poet Countee Cullen in 1928, it was a Harlem wedding like Negroes had never seen before, with sixteen bridesmaids and nine groomsmen!"

Lily feigned interest. Shirley continued.

"Here is the invitation that your Grandfather Alfred received. And look at this picture. Every Negro newspaper published it – *The Pittsburgh Courier, Atlanta Daily World, Amsterdam News* – all of them! Listen to how the papers described the wedding."

Lily began to get out of bed while Shirley read the newspaper clippings.

"Festoons of roses, carnations, sweet peas, and clinging vines with chirping songbirds in white cages and a large hovering white dove with outspread pinions."

"Sounds lovely, Mother," Lily groaned sarcastically. Her mother frequently talked about Yolande Du Bois's wedding, fantasizing that she, too, would have a wedding for her own daughter "the likes of which Little Rock had never seen before." Over the years, Lily's irritation with her mother's overbearing presence had slowly turned from tolerant to resentful.

Unfortunately, Lily's relationship with her parents, already complicated and tenuous, spiraled downward after her marriage. Rev. Frederick and Shirley Robinson never visited the couple in Pope City, and over time Lily and Joseph's visits to Little Rock became fewer and shorter. The last time Lily saw her father alive was during a Christmas visit to Little Rock. The extended Robinson family was seated for the annual dinner feast when her Aunt Alfreda from Detroit asked her brother and sister-in-law about the prospect of becoming grandparents. Loudmouthed and fast-talking, Aunt Alfreda teased Lily and Joseph about "getting the show on the road."

"Next Christmas, we got to have a baby at this table. Lily, you need me to draw you and Joseph a picture? Ya'll just need to relax and have some fun!"

No one laughed except Alfreda. Shirley picked up a serving dish and hurried into the kitchen.

The reverend was having none of it. He grabbed the napkin from his lap, slung it to the floor, and abruptly stood up.

"Alfreda, you keep that heathen talk out of my house!"

Now that his adrenalin was pumped up, Rev. Robinson couldn't seem to restrain himself. With all the fury he poured into his Sunday sermons, he turned to Lily.

"And I did not approve your marriage to this man! The Lord rebukes those who dishonor their father and mother. You will never be fruitful and multiply."

Lily jumped up from the table and bolted into her old room. She and Joseph packed and left for Pope City early the next morning. Three months later, Rev. Robinson had a heart attack and died. Her mother spent her last years, lonely and isolated, in Alfreda's basement in Detroit.

No one in Little Rock would have predicted such a dire ending to a member of the Robinson clan, a highfalutin family that had kept their noses up in the air while looking down on most people. They liked to brag that the Robinsons had never been slaves. "We're descendants of *free* Negroes," they'd say immodestly. When complimented about their clothes or possessions, the response was never *thank you.* Instead, they'd boast, "You can't find this in Little Rock. We shop in Detroit." And indeed, every August the Robinsons took the train to visit their Detroit kinfolk. They'd return with fancy clothes, inflated egos, and a resolve to maintain their status as the biggest fish in the small pond that was Little Rock. They were convinced that they were exceptional, and they never let anyone forget it.

In 1910, Lily's grandfather, Alfred Robinson, started the first Negro bank in Arkansas. He was an astute, albeit unscrupulous, businessman who knew that white bankers wouldn't lend Negroes a dime, so he took advantage of racism and segregation to build his fortune off poor people's Christmas club savings accounts, the high-interest loans they took out for everything from bail money to mortgages, and their repossessed houses. Although he called each customer by name, greeted them with a toothy smile and firm handshake, and inquired about their family's well-being, the community found little comfort in knowing that a Negro banker was exploiting them instead of a white one.

Alfred Robinson's large two-story house, perched brazenly on a steep hill, was more splendid than some of the homes owned by the town's white upper crust. The house was a must-see tourist stop for Negroes who traveled back and forth to Chicago or Detroit on "Blues" Highway 61. Its exterior looked like one of the miniature snow-covered houses in the Christmas window of Blass Department Store, complete with scalloped shingles, arched transoms, stained-glass windows, a paneled mahogany door, and wraparound porch. The porch served as a type of throne where the two generations of Robinsons who lived in the house literally and metaphorically looked down on their neighbors as they passed by.

Like the family that lived in the house, its fancy exterior masked a defective interior. There were uneven hardwood floors in the dining room where no one dined, plastic coverings on the sitting room furniture where no one sat, and a wood-paneled office where no one transacted business. The house sat on a two-acre lot on which no decent plant claimed home, and people wondered out loud why such a picture-book looking house had no zinnias, azaleas, roses, or hydrangea in the front yard. The backyard had a peculiar, sad vibe. The pecan trees would hang heavy with ripened nuts that no one ever ate, the limbs of the mature oak trees bent low to greet children but were never climbed.

There were so many opinions about how Lily's grandfather Alfred had acquired his house that the family ultimately decided that the truth didn't matter. Lily's father, Rev. Frederick Robinson, told his congregants at Mt. Zion African Methodist Episcopal (AME) that an angel had appeared in the middle of the night and commanded his father to build a beautiful house on a high hill "as a light unto the world." Even for his church members who lived in modest, overcrowded frame homes and aspired to a more affluent life, the reverend's story was hard to swallow.

His sister, Lily's Aunt Alfreda in Detroit, said that her daddy built the house as revenge against the mean, wealthy white folks who had mistreated his family. The story was widely known in Alfreda's church and social circles, and she never missed an opportunity to share it whenever she found a captive audience.

"You see," she would say, "even when he was a little boy, Daddy had a dream. He said he was gonna open a bank and build a house that looked exactly like the white folks' houses his mama and poppa worked in. And you know, that's exactly what he did! Ain't bragging, just telling you what happened. My folks always stepped in high cotton."

To emphasize her point, she would place one hand on her hip and wave the other in the air as if to proclaim, "I am somebody!"

"When those crackers saw their former maid and yard man living in a replica of their own home, they burned their house down and left town in disgrace."

Everybody took Alfreda's unlikely story for what it was: When Negroes moved up North, they told exaggerated accounts about oppression down South, and when Negroes made their reunion trips to the South, they told even more exaggerated tales about prosperity in the North.

Depending on whether the setting was a church or a Masonic event, Lily's father was called Reverend Doctor or First Worshipful Master. And worship was precisely what her father and his wife expected. Lily's mother was never called Shirley or Mrs. Robinson. She was reverently addressed as First Lady. It was bad enough that Negroes bowed and scraped to avoid the wrath of racist white folks, but the idea that a Negro family acted like African royalty and expected "Uncle Tom" behavior from its own people was an even more egregious insult.

First Lady was forever pleasant and insufferably boring. More comfortable around children than adults, she was the Sunday school superintendent and the Sunbeam children's choir director. As a member of the Negro aristocracy, she believed it was her duty to uplift the race by teaching ignorant and uncultured children the proper etiquette of the Negro middle class. She also saw her husband's church as the perfect training ground for her daughter's future as a member of Fisk University's Jubilee Singers. Even though Lily was just a toddler, First Lady had decided that her daughter would attend her alma mater, become a featured singer in Fisk's famed choral ensemble, and one day perform for dignitaries around the world.

In addition to directing the children's choir, First Lady was the writer, composer, producer, and director of every platitudinous and pedestrian Christmas pageant, Easter play, and Youth Sunday skit. Mt. Zion members watched Lily star in every performance from the age of two to sixteen. While the other Sunbeam girls wore homemade or hand-me-down green skirts and ill-fitting white blouses with shiny paper ribbon belts salvaged from old Christmas wrappings, Lily's appearance was always stunning. Dressed in one of her ornate dresses from Detroit, Lily's hair was styled in freshly pressed Shirley Temple curls with cut bangs that stayed properly rolled throughout the performance. She didn't wear a construction paper name tag around her neck to identify her role like the children who played angels or centurions or Pharisees. Instead, she had her own byline in the printed program, *Special Performance By.* None of these affronts to the congregation was as heart-wrenching as the fact that Lily, who could actually sing, was always given some spiritless, European music to sing, like Bach's cantata, *Jesu, Joy of Man's Desiring*, a monotonous song that could drive the most pious church mother to drink.

* * * * *

Lily and her parents hugged and exchanged pleasantries during the short ride to Fisk University Memorial Chapel. As the parents of the bride, Rev. Frederick and Shirley Robinson were polite to Joseph's parents, Rev. Joseph and Elmira Washington, and to the couple's small group of friends.

Walking down the aisle with her father, Lily caught a glimpse of her mother. Heartbroken to be sitting in the unadorned chapel, she was wiping away tears as she watched her plans for a spectacular wedding vanish, just as had most of her dreams. Rev. Robinson's grim expression was more fitting for a funeral procession than for his daughter's wedding. He had his own hopes and had prayed for a lawyer or doctor son-in-law from a noted northern family.

Soon after the wedding, the newlyweds headed south for their new life in Joseph's hometown of Pope City, Georgia, a place Lily knew nothing about. They moved into the parsonage of Payne

Chapel AME Church with Joseph's parents. Joseph was hired to teach Social Studies at the local high school and to direct the school's chorus. Lily taught elementary school and earned extra money giving private piano lessons. Both volunteered at Joseph's father's church to lead the First Sunday Choir that sang for Communion services, the least dreadful of the church's singing groups. There were no auditions for Payne Chapel choirs. Only three qualifications were required: attend evening choir rehearsal every third Monday of the month, keep your choir robe cleaned and pressed, and be able to read or memorize the songs in the AME hymnal. The lack of talent didn't really matter since Joseph and Lily did most of the singing.

Lily was fond of her new family. Joseph was like his parents – thoughtful, caring, humble, and soft-spoken. Lily enjoyed spending time with Mrs. Washington, who taught her how to garden, bake, and crochet. Most importantly, she taught Lily that Negro women could be both gracious and assertive. Her mother-in-law was definitely in charge. She organized the household and all of Rev. Washington's church business. Lily was only uncomfortable around her in-laws when they teased about becoming grandparents. She and Joseph had been married for two years and hadn't conceived, and she couldn't stop worrying.

"Stop worrying so much. We'll have a family one day," Joseph said encouragingly. "Why don't we do something to take our minds off it, take a road trip? Fisk's homecoming is in two weeks. We should go and have some fun. Say yes and I'll work out the details."

Lily saw that her husband needed a break as much as she did so she reluctantly agreed. Traveling through the segregated South was dangerous, which meant that Joseph would have to carefully map out their route. It was not uncommon to hear about vacationing Negro families confronted by the Ku Klux Klan on lonely back roads in "sundown" towns where signs posted along the highways warned, *Nigger, don't let the sun go down on you in this town.* So, they would travel in the daylight and stop only for gas. Since there were no restaurants where they could sit down to eat, Lily packed a lunch. Fortunately, the four-hour trip to Nashville wouldn't require an overnight stay on the road. Once in Nashville, they would be able to find a room in one of the few Black-owned hotels. The getaway did them both good, and they made other brief trips to Tuskegee, Mobile, and Jacksonville.

Lily's spirits were also lifted by the friendship she was developing with Ruby Harper. Miss Ruby, as people called her, was the wife of the AME district's Presiding Elder, Rev. Robert Harper. In their official capacities as church leaders, the reverend and his wife visited all the AME churches within a 75-mile radius of his district. Rev. Washington's church hosted the Presiding Elder every fifth Sunday. Payne Chapel's combined choirs sang, the senior usher board served, the most articulate church member gave the welcome, and the old deacons chimed in emphatically with *Amen!* and *Yes, Lord!* After church, the Washingtons would host dinner in their home for Rev. and Mrs. Harper, a much-anticipated affair that required days of planning and preparation by Lily and Mrs. Washington.

Elder Harper was short and half white. One might have expected him to have a light-skinned, rail-thin, deferential wife like Lily's mother, but that wasn't Miss Ruby. She was tall, had a dark complexion, had considerable "meat on her bones," and spoke her mind. Her husband was one of the most respected and affluent men in the community. He owned hundreds of acres of land, streets of rental houses, a construction business, and several "mom and pop" cinderblock stores. His church work and businesses kept him away from home most of the time. He left home after Miss Ruby fixed his 6:00 a.m. breakfast and returned for his 7:00 p.m. dinner. By 8:00 p.m., he was nodding off on the sofa in front of the potbelly stove and was in bed by 9:00 p.m.

The Harpers lived in the Poplar Springs section of Pope City. They had four children and, unlike Lily's parents, they lived modestly, never "putting on airs" or feeling superior to the less fortunate. They never evicted their renters, and Miss Ruby took money out of her husband's cash box when neighbors fell on hard times. She cared about everyone the same – the "saved," the "unsaved," the young, the old, the educated, the illiterate, the married, the divorced, and the unmarried mother. She held no disdain for poor people or any admiration for the wealthy. Miss Ruby was soft-spoken, but her strong character and nurturing nature spoke volumes about who she was.

One of the legendary stories about Miss Ruby involved the local outcast, Jerry, a dull-witted and harmless old man who cleaned outhouses. His dark skin blended with the black-stained, wide-brimmed hat he wore cocked to the side in a futile effort to cover his right eye, a narrow slit with no eyeball. He wore overalls with straps attached by huge safety pins, shirts with missing sleeves, and shit-covered boots with no socks or shoelaces. He didn't walk; he shuffled. He didn't talk; he mumbled. He transported his stinky shovels and bucket on a loud, rusty, lopsided Radio Flyer wagon he had retrieved from the city dump. He was the only adult man in the community that children were allowed to call by his first name. Apparently, he didn't deserve the salutation *Mister.*

Everybody had a horror story about Jerry: he stole misbehaving children in the middle of the night and threw them in the river, he patted little girls on the butt and rubbed little boys' penises, he dug up dead bodies. No matter the source of the information or the improbability of the tale, whenever Jerry showed up, women called the children inside and latched their screen doors. But no one passed up the opportunity to gawk at him.

One Saturday afternoon, Miss Ruby was busy preparing dinner for the bishop's quarterly Sunday visit. Her two oldest girls, Lucille and Eula, had been given the task of cleaning the living room. That was Miss Ruby's special room for company, and her children were seldom allowed there. The room was dominated by a brown stuffed camel-back sofa with claw feet. Its arms were covered with white linen antimacassars with crocheted floral trims. The window behind the sofa was covered with heavy brown drapes that had a pink rose design.

Sitting on the coffee table in front of the sofa were Depression glass candy dishes lined with starched crocheted doilies and loaded with hard candy. Above the damask wing chair was a wall-mounted corner shelf that displayed miniature ceramic knick-knacks – miniature cups and saucers, a circus dog on its hind legs with a ring in its mouth, a white ballerina, a family of kittens, and Rudolph, the red-nosed reindeer.

Ruby was at work in the dining room. She had polished silverware, cleaned the "good" glasses, washed, starched, and ironed her lace-trimmed white linen tablecloth and napkins, and now she was taking her good dishes out of the china cabinet. Her children were always amused by the care she took with dishes they rarely ate on and usually only saw through the glass door of the cabinet. Miss Ruby had just started setting the table when she heard someone cry, "Miss Ruby, Miss Ruby!" She walked to the screen door and saw the neighbor's little girl running up her back steps.

"Miss Ruby," she said, trying to catch her breath, "dem boys is chuckin' rocks at Jerry. He done fell down and can't get up."

Miss Ruby rushed up the street. By the time she got there, Jerry had managed to sit up. The teen boys scattered when they saw her, and the neighbors gathered nearby to see what Miss Ruby was going to do.

"Mister Jerry," she asked, "you thirsty?" He nodded. "Okay," she said, "stay here. I'll be right back."

Miss Ruby rushed back to her house. When she came back, she was holding one of her "good" glasses full of ice water and a starched white linen napkin retrieved from the dining room table she had set for the bishop and his wife.

"Here," Miss Ruby said, bending down to Jerry, "take your time. Hard as you work, you need some rest."

Everyone was in shock, and the gossipy women couldn't wait to spread the news that Miss Ruby had lost her mind. They may not have realized it at that moment, but Miss Ruby had just preached the best sermon anyone in Pope City had ever heard. No one ever bothered Mister Jerry again.

* * * * *

Lily admired Miss Ruby and tried to visit at least once a month. She drove Miss Ruby, her mother-in-law, and other church mothers to district missionary meetings and to the homes of the sick and shut-in. She sat on Miss Ruby's screened-in porch and they chatted about the mundane happenings in the community while mindlessly shelling peas, snapping green beans, or cleaning greens. Miss Ruby always sat in the metal glider with her fly swatter and ice water nearby. Lily preferred the swaying porch swing. The feeling of being suspended in the air calmed her and reminded her of the swing on her parents' porch in Little Rock. Their mundane chitchat turned more serious during one pea-shelling session. Lily looked down at the pile of peas in her lap.

"I don't think I'll ever have a baby," she whispered. "I've been praying and trying to hold on to my faith, but I'm getting discouraged."

"Oh, Lily, you have to believe. Never give up. The Lord answers prayers, but not always as you might expect. So, we'll both keep praying."

Lily always left Miss Ruby's house with a renewed spirit along with an armful of seedlings, cuttings, flowers, or vegetables from her impressive gardens. Miss Ruby's gardens were metaphors for how she lived and how she raised her children. Each flower was special and deserved her care. In her resolve to transform barren land into beauty, she braved rain, drought, insects, and sun. She never wavered. No droopy, half-dead stem was tossed away. Ruby believed anything could thrive if you kept nurturing it.

The Harpers had four beautiful children – Lucille, Eula, Junior, and Margaret. The oldest daughter, Lucille, only ten years younger than Lily, was the darkest of the children and wasn't particularly friendly. Lily never saw her smile, and she always seemed preoccupied with her chores. Eula, the next oldest, just followed her older sister's directives. When Lily visited, they would mumble their obligatory *hellos* before returning to their housekeeping. The third born child, Junior, was seldom home.

"Miss Ruby," Lily asked during one visit, "where's Junior? Haven't seen him in a while."

Miss Ruby looked down at her folded hands and seemed troubled. "Somewhere playing, I guess. You know how boys is. Always into somethin.'"

After that, Lily stopped bringing up his name.

The youngest of Miss Ruby's children was a "late" baby, Margaret, who was born when Miss Ruby was thirty-five years old. Her behavior was a bit peculiar, and she didn't talk or interact much with her siblings. In her education classes at Fisk, Lily had learned about children who had learning difficulties or were regarded as feeble-minded by the community. However, Margaret didn't have any of the distorted physical features like a flattened face or small, deep-set eyes that those children typically did. Margaret was beautiful. Nonetheless, Lily was sure that something wasn't quite right with Margaret.

One morning when Lily stopped by to pick up Miss Ruby to take her to a "sick and shut-in" visit, Margaret was playing in the front yard by herself. While she waited for Miss Ruby to finish getting ready, she stayed outside with Margaret, who was baking a mud cake. Margaret scooped up and dumped some dirt in an empty Crisco oil can and then took the can over to the outdoor faucet to catch some of the dripping water. Sitting back down on the ground, she stirred the "batter" until it had the right consistency, patted it down with her fist until it was firm, and then quickly flipped the can over onto a piece of cardboard. The cake fell out intact.

Lily clapped. "Good job, Margaret!" Margaret smiled and jumped up and down. Lily concluded that Margaret could learn. She had obviously watched this routine and could repeat it. "It's such a beautiful cake, Margaret. Let's decorate it!"

Lily took a leaf from a tree, a few small twigs from the ground, and pinched off one of Miss Ruby's flowers. Margaret did the same and immediately started arranging them on her cake. Lily was curious to see if she could get Margaret to talk.

"What's that?" Lily asked, pointing to the cake. Margaret looked but didn't respond. Lily slowly repeated the word: "Cake. Cake. Cake." When Margaret still didn't answer, Lily asked, "Do you like to cook?" Margaret enthusiastically nodded her head.

Just then, Miss Ruby opened the screen door and headed down the steps. Margaret ran and grabbed her mother's leg.

"Mama, Mama," Margaret said excitedly and pointed to the cake.

"You are Mama's *best* cook! Now go in the house with your sisters, baby. I'll be back soon."

This was the first time that Lily had ever heard Margaret's voice, and she wanted to interact with her more, perhaps teach her, but she never got the chance.

The monthly visits to Miss Ruby's home changed over time and became less frequent. When she'd stop by, she'd get a strange reception. One time Eula came to the door and said that her mother was sleeping, which was unusual because Miss Ruby never slept in the middle of the day. Another time no one answered the door, even though Lily heard movement and whispers coming from the house. The last time she knocked on the door, Miss Ruby answered but did not unlatch the screen door. Her appearance was shocking. She looked like she had lost fifteen pounds. Her hair was uncombed, and her eyes were swollen.

"Miss Ruby," Lily said, hoping her shock didn't show in her face, "What's wrong? Are you okay?"

"Lily," Miss Ruby said wearily, "I'm sorry but come back in a few weeks. I got a lot on my mind right now."

Without saying goodbye, Miss Ruby closed the door. Lily cried as she drove home. Lord, she prayed, please take care of Miss Ruby.

Joseph, meanwhile, had started spending more time in his father's church. He was elected to the trustee board, served as a delegate to the AME state conference, and became leader of the men's Bible study group. As his involvement got deeper, he would have long, private conversations with his father, Presiding Elder Harper, and the bishop for their district.

One evening after dinner, Joseph told Lily that he had passed up an opportunity to apply for the recently vacant position of assistant principal at the high school where he was teaching. Lily was surprised.

"Why would you pass up such a great opportunity? What's going on?" she asked.

Joseph reached across the table and took hold of Lily's hand.

"Honey, like my father and grandfather, I've been called to the ministry. I've tried *not* to walk down this path, but I always end up at the same place. I want to be an ordained minister."

Lily was incensed. A preacher's daughter herself, she had seen her father use his authority for his own selfish ends, treat people who he decided were "beneath" him with contempt, and take advantage of his congregation. She had had enough of preachers. If Joseph had expressed his interest in the ministry when they were dating, she wasn't sure she would have married him.

Plodding on despite the angry look on his wife's face, Joseph mapped out the plan he and the bishop had discussed. The AME church had started sending bishops and missionaries to Africa in 1890 and had four districts on the continent. Joseph would study to become an AME missionary in Accra, Ghana. Certification for the Africa assignment required six months of study at the AME Theology and Missionary Training Institute in Gary, Indiana. The bishop was offering free travel and housing, a teaching job for Lily at one of the local Accra elementary schools in Gary, and, if Lily wished, occasional tutoring work at the AME orphanage.

Joseph paused after the word "orphanage."

"You see, Lily," he continued, "this move to Africa is the answer to all our prayers. We can live independent of my folks, see the world, and meet different kinds of people. And it gives us time to decide if the ministry is right for me and where the next phase of our lives should take us. But more than anything, Lily, we can adopt a baby from the orphanage. Two babies, three! As many as you like! This vision has been revealing itself in my dreams for months. Please, think about it."

Lily just frowned. They seldom disagreed and rarely raised their voices, but now she was ready to cuss him out. Not only was he toying with the idea of going into the ministry which he knew she was against, but he was also giving up on them conceiving a child of their own. She stared at him, dumfounded.

"Who knows about this silly plan?" she asked.

"No one," he said. "Take your time. Think about it. Pray over it. I'm not pressuring you to do anything you don't want to do. I love you and would never do anything that made you unhappy."

For weeks, Lily couldn't talk about "the plan," and Joseph didn't ask her about it. She felt angry, scared, and, most of all, confused. On the one hand, there were some positives to the plan. The move would fulfill Lily's dream to travel without depleting their hard-earned savings. And even though she hoped that Joseph wouldn't go into the ministry, he had a right to find his career path just as she wanted to find hers. Perhaps most importantly, she and Joseph had spent their entire adult lives either in a Fisk dorm or under Joseph's parents' roof. She was yearning to live independently and preferably far away.

There was one major negative, though. She would never adopt an African baby. First of all, there were no orphanages for Negro children in the segregated South, so the idea of adopting an institutionalized child was foreign to Lily. She knew about families who "took in" their relatives' children when, for example, the mother died or couldn't care for them. But these arrangements didn't involve white folks, their courts, their paperwork, or their approval. The idea of trying to negotiate this unfamiliar territory in a foreign country was overwhelming. Besides, Lily had never seen an African baby, child, or adult in Pope City or Nashville. When Lily asked Joseph if he had ever heard of an AME member adopting an African child, he replied in his typical Pollyannaish way, "Well, we'll be the first!"

Lily loved Joseph because of his optimistic attitude about life. However, he could also be downright naïve.

Joseph's parents were not at all supportive when Lily and Joseph shared their thoughts about going to Ghana. Mrs. Washington cried and predicted dire outcomes – animal attacks, uncivilized "natives," straw huts, and incurable diseases. Rev. Washington was equally pessimistic but mostly he was angry that Joseph hadn't sought his advice and permission.

"Daddy, I'm a grown man," Joseph reminded his father, "and my wife and I will decide ourselves what's best for us. I'm not asking for permission. I'm just hoping that you'll support us as we explore our options for the future."

It was in that moment that Lily knew she would follow her husband to Africa if that's where he wanted to go.

The relocation process progressed more quickly than Lily had anticipated and required a complicated and exhausting itinerary: a train to Atlanta where they would catch another train to Gary, Indiana; six months at the Bible College and Missionary Center, at the end of which they would take a train to New York; a ship from New York would take them to London, and they would take a plane from there to Accra, Ghana.

They only had forty days to get to Gary for the start of the next missionary training, and there was so much to do. At the top of Lily's list, though, was to go see Miss Ruby before she heard the news from someone else. The AME church had a gossip grapevine that operated more efficiently than Bell Telephone Company, the US postal service, trans-Atlantic cables, and Western Union combined. Although Atlanta was just 100 miles away, most Pope City folks had never been there, and Africa was like another planet to them. The grapevine would be busy!

Lily was troubled by what she saw as she made her way to Miss Ruby's door. The flowers and vegetables that had once burst with color and vitality now looked lackluster. For the first time, she spotted weeds. She didn't hear the familiar sounds of Miss Ruby humming or Lucille and Eula moving about with their cleaning. The cat that Lily couldn't stand didn't crawl out from under the house to greet her. When Miss Ruby opened the door, Lily's heart sank. No welcoming smile or smothering hug or cheerful greeting. No offer of food or something to drink.

Lily followed Miss Ruby onto the screened-in porch and took her usual seat on the swing. There was an awkward silence. Making a half-hearted attempt to appear normal, Miss Ruby asked, "So, what's been going on?"

"I came to see how you're doing and to share some good news," Lily said, hoping she sounded more chipper than she felt.

"I need some good news. I'm just waiting patiently on the Lord to give me a sign. To see me through this storm—"

Lily knew where this conversation was heading. Miss Ruby was getting wound up to deliver one of her sermonettes. Lily leaned in closer and politely interrupted. She wanted to stay on track.

Lily told Miss Ruby about Joseph's vision, their impending departure to Africa, and her in-laws' disapproval. Even Miss Ruby looked distressed when she described the long, complex itinerary. She also told Miss Ruby about Joseph's preposterous idea of adopting a baby in Africa. When she noticed that Miss Ruby was staring at the top of a nearby chinaberry tree and didn't seem to be listening, Lily assumed that she had lost interest, so she stopped talking about the trip and asked Ms. Ruby about her gardens. She didn't answer.

"Miss Ruby? Miss Ruby, are you OK?"

When Miss Ruby still didn't answer, Lily began to get nervous. Finally, after several minutes, Miss Ruby slowly turned to face Lily.

"The Bible says you have to be still in the presence of the Lord," Miss Ruby stated matter-of-factly. "Did you say ya'll got to first stop in Gary for six months? Where is that?"

"It's not far from Chicago, Miss Ruby. Just about 30 miles."

"That's what I thought, close to Chicago."

Miss Ruby smiled as tears suddenly began to slowly roll down her cheeks. She dabbed her eyes with her apron. Lily had never seen Miss Ruby cry before.

Miss Ruby stood up and shouted, "Lily, never forget God's amazing grace! Grace, grace, grace. Nothing but God's amazing grace!" Didn't I tell you that the Lord answers prayers but not always as you expect. Then she sang a line from the hymn in a very joyful voice: *Grace has brought me safe thus far, and grace will lead me home.*

These were the last words that Lily would ever hear Miss Ruby speak.

CHAPTER THREE

ACCRA, GHANA
NASHVILLE, TENNESSEE

As soon as missionaries Joseph and Lily Robinson Washington landed in Accra, Ghana in 1949, Lily wired her family. Landed safely yesterday. Good news. I'm having a baby. Will write a longer letter soon.

One of the stories that Lily would later tell her family and friends in the States was that when she arrived in Africa and found out she was pregnant, she was sure it was a sign from God.

"I was twenty-seven years old and thought I couldn't have a baby. I named her Neema, which means 'grace' in Swahili, because I believed that it was God's amazing grace that had answered Joseph's and my prayers. I didn't know then what He had in store for us."

Neema was a healthy, beautiful baby. Having been only children themselves, neither Lily nor Joseph knew exactly what to do with or expect from their eight-pound bundle of joy. They thought everything that Neema did was nothing less than a miracle. Lily, however, was a nervous and over-protective new mother.

"Joseph," she'd lament, "what's wrong with Baby Neema? She doesn't cry a lot like other babies." Then, when Neema cried, Lily would pace the floor, rocking the fretful infant in her arms. "Why is she crying, Joseph?"

Joseph's answer was always the same: "Guess because she's a baby."

Without a doubt, the most frequent comments that the Washingtons got about their baby were on her physical appearance. By the time Neema was six months old, her hair was so long that Lily could make three curly braids, one at the top of her little head and two on the sides, and women were constantly complimenting her. What got just as many comments was her complexion. Few of the townspeople had seen a baby whose skin color was so dissimilar to that of both parents. When anyone mustered up the nerve to ask about Neema's light skin, Lily and Joseph would explain, "She looks like her maternal grandmother."

Neema was a precocious baby. At three months, she was rolling over, and at six months, trying to sit up. She was so anxious to see the world that she never crawled. One day, when she was nine months old, Neema just stood up and started walking. Joseph couldn't wait to brag about his baby girl.

"She's only nine months old and can walk! She seldom cries, and she smiles *all* the time! What do you think about that?"

Not surprisingly, the responses to Joseph's mostly rhetorical question were as expected.

"Praise God! Such a smart baby!"

"You are blessed, brother. Cannot wait to see what she's gonna do next!"

"Yes, she's adorable."

When Joseph arrived in Accra, Turner Mission AME church had twenty members. It was a small, unimpressive, wood frame building that had been built in 1930. It sat on a concrete foundation and its exterior walls were clad in aluminum siding. Three arched windows adorned each side of the building. A louvered bell tower on top of the pitched roof held a tall wooden cross whose disproportionate size made the building look uncomfortably top-heavy.

Five concrete steps led to the entrance. The walls inside were painted white and the floors were covered in red carpeting. Pews were arranged around a center aisle – ten hand-carved, six-foot, backless benches on each side. Three steps in the front led to the altar and pulpit, behind which there was a small choir loft. The cramped space could barely accommodate the scratched, out-of-tune piano. Hanging high above the choir loft on the back wall was a faded picture of a white Jesus wearing a crown of thorns. Reflecting on the threadbare look of the church and its small membership, Lily teasingly called it the Have Mercy Mission. Joseph didn't think the barb was funny.

The AME church provided Joseph and his family with housing, a small parsonage that sat next to the church. Apparently, the house was built at the same time as the church – same concrete steps, same aluminum siding, same concrete foundation. The sparsely furnished three-bedroom house accommodated the essentials. The largest bedroom was furnished with a metal frame double bed, a chifforobe, and a chair. One of the church members had placed a straw baby basket beside the bed for Neema. The other two bedrooms each had a single bed, a table, and shelves on one wall. Lily and Joseph's missionary training had prepared them for their sparse living quarters. Being from Pope City, Georgia, Joseph had seen similar houses growing up. Lily, who hailed from the much bigger city of Little Rock, Arkansas, hadn't. But the young couple was excited about their new home and new beginnings and felt blessed to have an indoor bathroom. Most of their neighbors did not.

Joseph worked seven days a week on increasing the church's membership. His favorite outreach strategy was to participate in local community projects. He usually first approached the neighborhood elders to ask if he could help. Then for weeks on end he would work side-by-side with the men in the community shoveling dirt for a well or whatever the project was. He made sure that everyone understood that he was with the AME church and not with the World Bank or any of the other US and European agencies that many locals distrusted. He would come home exhausted, sore, and dirty, but his hard work slowly began to pay off. More people started to come to Turner Mission AME to worship.

Lily supported Joseph by completing the paperwork required for the church's district office. She also enjoyed organizing and directing the new choir that sang traditional AME hymns as well as local tribal songs of worship. But now that Neema was almost a year old, she would soon have to report to the second-grade teaching assignment that the AME bishop's office had secured for her. With so much to do, Lily and Joseph quickly realized they needed help.

Lily had noticed that one of their newer church members always sat alone and did not appear to have any family or close friends. She was an attractive young woman, perhaps in her late teens, who spoke when spoken to but avoided eye contact and seldom smiled. She seemed to be a responsible, level-headed person, and so Lily asked her if she wanted a job caring for Baby Neema and helping with the housework in the parsonage. The young woman quickly agreed and turned out to be the answer to their prayers.

The Washingtons called their new family member Aunt Eni, an Akan term meaning mother's sister. She had her own room, received a salary, and had weekends to herself. Aunt Eni went about her chores each day with Baby Neema tied on her back with colorful batik fabric. Neema played with the local children and over time learned to speak basic Akan and Twi. When she got older, she would happily escort Aunt Eni on her daily trips to Makola Market. Neema was a non-stop chatter box, engaging everyone she could: "What's your name?" "What's that?" "Want to see me dance?" Aunt Eni and Neema also took long walks along the shore of Labadi Beach and watched the men gracefully cast their fishing nets into the Gulf of Guinea.

As the Turner Mission's membership grew, so did the respect that the people in the neighborhoods in and around Accra had for the Washington family – Baba Joseph, Mama Lily, Baby Neema, and Aunt Eni.

For Neema's fourth birthday in 1954, her parents promised her a big celebration. It would be her first party where the guests included people other than her parents and Aunt Eni. She got to decide on the guest list and helped Aunt Eni bake a three-layer chocolate cake. On the much-anticipated day, Joseph moved tables from inside the church to a shady spot outside. Lily brought out the chairs, arranged them around the tables, and then helped Eni set and decorate the tables. The exhausting work was almost finished when Joseph heard a loud crash inside the church.

"Lily! Lily, what's going on in there?"

When he didn't get an answer, he rushed into the sanctuary, followed by Aunt Eni. Lily was lying unconscious on the floor. Aunt Eni turned and whisked Neema away before she could see anything.

"Lily, what's wrong?" Joseph said as he gently shook her shoulder. "Lily, Lily! Wake up!" He shook her again, a bit more roughly this time. "Lord, please don't take Lily from me!"

Lily's eyes fluttered open, and she slowly turned her head to face Joseph.

"Oh, Joseph," she whispered, "don't you worry. I'll be fine. Just tired, is all. Take me home so I can rest."

Although Joseph wanted to cancel Neema's party, Lily convinced him that he and Aunt Eni should go ahead without her. She didn't want to disappoint her baby.

The next day Joseph drove Lily to their doctor's office. At age thirty-one and with no significant health issues, Lily assured Joseph that there was probably nothing to be alarmed about.

"Don't worry, Joseph. I think I've just taken on too much with my teaching job and church duties and being a wife and mother. I promise, I'll scale back."

As Joseph waited for the doctor to finish seeing Lily, he prayed for the best, but when a solemn nurse said the doctor wanted to see him in the examination room, he was prepared for the worst. To his great relief, Lily was sitting on the exam table with a big smile on her face.

"Joseph, I'm three months pregnant! We're gonna have a baby in March!"

The couple was overjoyed by Lily's unexpected pregnancy. Neema was even more excited and informed everyone in her constant singsong chant, "I'm going to be a big sister, big sister, big sister."

Lily's pregnancy was difficult. In addition to morning sickness, she experienced severe headaches, swollen feet, varicose veins, and dizziness. In order to keep Lily entertained, Joseph started the Lily and Joseph Book Club. They would request "care packages" from relatives in the States – newspaper clippings from *The Pittsburgh Courier*, copies of *Jet* magazine, and the latest books by important African American writers.

The first book to arrive was a 1952 publication by Ralph Ellison, *Invisible Man*. Lily was critical of Ellison's description of Dr. Bledsoe, the fictional president of a Negro college in the South.

"I don't think a Negro college president, even one lacking in judgment and integrity, would exile a student to an awful place like New York," Lily said. "And the description of the college is not my experience. So much violence and depravity!"

"Calm down, Lily," Joseph said. "You don't have to get personal and defensive about the book. Besides, you're a third-generation college graduate. Don't know if you can really relate to how this Negro man felt. White people don't allow us men to be visible. So maybe you're missing the point."

"No," she countered, "you're missing the point! We are *both* invisible and abused Negroes. Pain has no gender."

Every book or article they read together opened the door to an intense but friendly debate. Lily was not one to back down or defer, and neither was Joseph.

One day, Neema listened as her parents discussed a book that had just arrived from the States. "Why can't Aunt Eni be in the book club?" she asked.

Joseph and Lily looked at each other but did not answer. "That's not fair," the persistent Neema observed. "People are supposed to share. Right?"

"Aunt Eni is very busy," Joseph mumbled.

As expected, Neema marched into the kitchen and asked Aunt Eni if she wanted to read books with her parents. Eni politely refused, but Neema would regularly bring up the subject. After more than a few stern warnings, she finally stopped.

Lily and Joseph knew Eni could not read, but Eni never admitted it. In church, she opened the hymnal during responsive readings but never read. The fact that a young woman Eni's age could not read was unusual but not unheard of. Although Lily and Eni had a good relationship, Lily thought it best to wait for Eni to ask for help. She didn't want to embarrass her.

Weeks passed before Eni decided to talk about the book club incident. She spoke to Lily in a whispered voice when they were alone in the kitchen. "Mama Lily, I can't read."

"Eni, why didn't you go to school in your rural village?"

Eni stopped cooking, sat in a chair, and shared her painful story. "Mama Lily, I was born in a small village about fifty miles from here. I was the oldest of five children, and by the time I was eight years old, my mother had joined my father in the cocoa fields, the farms, or wherever they could find work. I kept my sisters and brothers from dawn until Mama and Papa came home in the late evenings. I cooked, washed, and kept house as good as a grown woman. By the time I was eleven, Daddy had lost his right leg in a machine accident. He got gangrene and died a few months later. We were having a hard time, and I don't blame Mama for what she did next. She had to do what she had to do. One day a man came by and gave Mama some money to take me to cure his sickness. The man had some kind of venereal disease, and back then people thought having sex with a virgin cured these kinds of problems. I caught the disease, and he kept coming back for me and paying Mama until I got pregnant. Mama Lily, I was just twelve years old. My son didn't make it. He died soon after he was born."

The two women cried as Eni continued. "When I turned fourteen, another older man whose wife died having a baby gave Mama money so he could take me for his wife. After two miscarriages, he kicked me out of his house and said I was no good. Said he needed a wife to bear his children. I had nowhere to go. I couldn't go back home, so I roamed the streets begging for food. But I refused to lay with men for money. I was going to starve before I did that!"

"Oh, Eni. I can't imagine what you have been through. I had no idea. Lord, have mercy."

"I thought things were looking up when a man approached me in the market one day and asked me if I needed a job. Said he knew people in Accra who were looking for maids to take care of their house and children. I said OK without asking any questions. So that's how I ended up here in Accra, practically a slave in that house. This was where I was working when you first saw me in Church. You and Baba Joseph saved my life. I am so blessed to have you. You have been so kind to me."

Lily was not naïve about conditions in Africa. However, hearing Eni tell her story was too close to home. Eni was a member of their family now. Lily did not know how to comfort Eni. She kept saying repeatedly, "I'm so sorry, I'm so sorry. I wish I could have been there to help you."

"Mama Lily don't cry. I'm fine now. But I do want you to help me with something."

"What do you need, Eni?"

"Please teach me to read. I really want to read."

Lily's resolve to teach Eni was the impetus to give her a new purpose in life. Every day after work and on Saturdays, she taught Eni to read. Eni practiced reading from Neema's books, the newspapers, the Bible, even words printed on items purchased at the market. Eni learned quickly and was not hesitant to show her church members her newly acquired reading skills. One Sunday, she surprised the congregation when she walked up the altar steps and read the Bible scripture for Joseph's sermon. The church rejoiced with applause and Amens.

Soon Lily was flooded with pleas from illiterate women in her church and community who also wanted to read. Lily was compelled to respond, so she started the Turner Mission AME Reading Center. Every Saturday morning, Lily and her small group of volunteer tutors, including Eni, taught Ghanaian women and girls how to read.

In her sixth month, Neema woke Joseph up in the middle of the night. "Joseph, when I went to the bathroom, I saw blood in the toilet."

Early the following day, Lily and Joseph saw the doctor, who diagnosed that Lily had high blood pressure and a weak cervix. He prescribed medications and strict bed rest, which meant that Lily could only leave her bed to go to the bathroom.

On March 30, 1955, seven-pound Kwame Joseph Washington unexpectedly made his grand entrance in Lily and Joseph's bed, not at the hospital as they had planned. With a head full of thick curly locks, the beautiful, brown boy was the best news the church community had heard since another church member had had twins the previous year. But no one was more excited than Neema. She would sneak into the baby's room to see if he was awake, and several times Lily caught her trying to wake him up. When Joseph held the baby, Neema would try to take Kwame out of his arms.

"Neema, please go away," Joseph would playfully chide. "You played with Kwame this morning. It's my turn!"

"I have three children on my hands," Lily would joke.

One month after Kwame was born, he was christened in a combined AME-traditional Ghanaian ceremony. Joseph officiated over the church ceremony. Lily held Kwame as Joseph proudly sprinkled his son while saying, "In the name of the Father, Son, and Holy Ghost." Four-year-old Neema, dressed in her first Kente cloth outfit, sang *Jesus Loves the Little Children*. Not known to lack self-confidence, she responded to the church's standing ovation by singing an unsolicited encore.

The Ghanaian "Outdooring," or Naming Ceremony as it was also known, took place after the service in the open space behind the church. Now dressed in a traditional Ghanaian Gonja smock, Joseph poured the libations and lifted his son toward the heavens.

"Most gracious and loving Father, I present to you Kwame Joseph Washington, the son of Joseph and Lily and the brother of Neema. He is named after Kwame Nkrumah, the father of Ghana's liberation movement and after Joseph, his father and grandfather. Thank you for this gift to us all. May this son of Africa and America represent the goodness and strength of his ancestors on both sides of the Atlantic. Lord, give this church family the wisdom to raise him in your amazing grace, knowledge, compassion, and love. Let the church say Amen."

Then the party began. The djembe and dondo drummers played first and were later joined by women dancers and, to everyone's delight, Neema. Lily proudly repeated, "Go, Neema, go!" as her daughter instinctively switched back and forth between polyrhythms, her arms moving to one beat and her legs to another. The festivities lasted for hours, and all agreed that the American couple had given Baby Kwame an acceptable Outdooring.

* * * * *

The loud noise of a passing truck woke Lily up on a rainy morning one month after Baby Kwame's naming ceremony. She glanced at the clock and was shocked to see that it was 7:00 a.m. She smiled. Thank goodness, she thought, my greedy boy has finally slept through the night. Not wanting to wake up Joseph, she carefully got out of bed to check on Kwame, figuring he'd be hungry soon since he'd missed his 3:00 a.m. feeding. She tiptoed over to his bassinette and lifted the mosquito netting. She smiled as she thought about her precious newborn. She reached out to rub his back when her heart skipped a beat. Something was wrong. Her baby wasn't breathing.

Lily's scream shook the parsonage like a blast of dynamite and reverberated out into the street. "No!" she yelled, and desperately tried to get her nonresponsive baby to latch onto her breast. Aunt Eni ran in to see what the ruckus was about. Joseph could only point to his wife rocking her cold, ashen baby boy. Eni wailed and ran for help.

For the first time in his life, Joseph felt that his faith had let him down. God had given his family an unexpected gift and then taken it away without warning or explanation. Lily held Kwame and hummed the hymn *Amazing Grace* until Eni returned with the doctor, who took the small body away.

Kwame Joseph Washington, like many children in Africa, had died from malaria. Just two months after celebrating his arrival, Turner Mission AME was now saying goodbye. The baby lay in a mahogany coffin that had been made by one of Accra's master craftsmen. The bassinette-shaped casket with carved hearts and baby angels seemed incongruous at a funeral. While hymns were sung, prayers delivered, and eulogy preached, Lily stared silently at the tiny coffin. Neema buried her face in her mother's lap, and Aunt Eni rocked back and forth, moaning. Joseph pretended to listen, but he didn't hear any of the funeral remarks. Kwame was buried in the cemetery behind the church. On his marker were the words, *An Angel Forever Loved.*

* * * * *

It took Joseph two months before he could focus on healing himself and his shattered family. He was physically present but emotionally absent, performed his ministerial duties by rote. Lily and Neema were out of school for summer break, but Lily stayed in bed most days, including Sundays, and rarely joined the family for meals. Neema stuck close to Aunt Eni and wasn't her usual playful self.

One Sunday morning, Aunt Eni told Joseph that Neema didn't want to get up to go to church. Concerned, Joseph went to check on her.

"Wake up, Neema, and put on your Sunday clothes. It's time to go to Sunday school."

"I don't feel good, Daddy."

Joseph looked into his daughter's eyes and felt her forehead, but he didn't see any signs of illness. "Does your stomach hurt?"

"No," Neema said, "I just don't wanna go. Mother *never* goes. Why do I have to?"

"Well," Joseph explained, "your mother is sick but you're not. I know you're missing your brother. We all are. But remember, he's in a better place, in heaven with God."

Neema was struggling to understand. "So, Kwame's happy," she asked as a tear rolled down her cheek, "and we're sad? Is it better to be dead than alive?"

Joseph was at a loss for words, and so he fell back on what he knew – faith.

"We may not understand why God does the things He does, but we have to have faith that He is right in all things."

Neema went to Sunday school that morning, but for the rest of her life she had doubts about God being right about *everything*.

The conversation with Neema prompted Joseph to do something counter to his natural inclinations. A few days later, he marched into his and Lily's bedroom with an armful of boxes.

"Get up, Lily! Kwame's clothes, this bassinette, the rocker, and all this baby stuff are headed to needy families in the villages. Our son is dead, but our daughter is alive. We're alive. We're all devastated, but we're moving forward, Lily. We have to for Neema's sake."

* * * * *

Three years passed, and slowly the pain of losing Kwame dulled. Apparently, "keep moving" was Lily's strategy for dealing with her grief. In addition to her teaching job and church duties, Lily accepted speaking engagements from local women's church groups and national Ghanaian civic organizations. She was always busy. Now seven years old, Neema lackadaisically participated in church activities when she had to, but school and extracurricular activities brought her the most joy. Whatever was going on, Neema Washington was in the middle of it – spelling bees, plays, choral recitals, dance recitals, essay contests, oratorical debates. When she didn't have after-school clubs or Saturday practices, she still liked to follow Aunt Eni to the street markets in downtown Accra, eavesdropping on the market women's conversations or dancing in impromptu street parades.

Joseph began to spend his free time under the town's largest baobab tree reading or debating with college students and intellectuals. The tree was nearly one hundred feet tall and twenty feet wide. Ghanaians believe that the baobab, which they refer to as the Tree of Life, has juju or magical powers that bestow wisdom, longevity, and strength. Joseph felt at home under the tree arguing with men of all ages.

They reminded him of the men in the Looking Good Barber Shop in his hometown of Pope City, where weekly Saturday haircuts evolved into raucous four-hour debates about some esoteric point that no one remembered by the time they got home.

The educated Africans were impatient nation-builders committed to change. Although Ghana had its share of problems with tribalism, nepotism, and poverty, its people were proud and industrious. Above all else, what Ghanaians in the 1950s wanted was a national identity, self-determination, and free education for all. Joseph was incredibly impressed with the courage of Kwame Nkrumah, a revolutionary leader who had attended a historically Black college (HBCU) in America. One of Joseph's parishioners gave him a used copy of Nkrumah's 1945 pamphlet, *Toward Colonial Freedom*. Joseph was inspired and always kept a quote from Nkrumah in his office: *It is far better to be free to govern or misgovern yourself than to be governed by anyone else.*

Despite the camaraderie under the baobab tree, Joseph knew that he was an interloper, and he wasn't offended. No one asked about his family, his church, or his past. Occasionally, the men would exclude him by speaking in their tribal language. He was never invited to their homes or to their "war room" meetings where they discussed Nkrumah and his Convention People's Party's plan to overthrow the British colonial government and gain majority rule in Parliament. He understood that serious discussions like that needed to be kept secret from outsiders. Along with everyone else in the country, he celebrated when, on March 6, 1957, Ghana gained its independence, and Kwame Nkrumah became the first president.

One summer morning in 1958, a tall, bearded African American man strutted toward the baobab, sat on the periphery, and listened to the debate *du jour*. He was dressed in a dashiki and perfectly pressed pants, but his wool tam and Stacy Adams shoes screamed his recent arrival in Accra. His name was John Bogle, and he was savvy enough to wait until the baobab group invited him into the conversation. Joseph quickly realized that his own stories about Fisk University and Pope City were boring and sophomoric compared to Bogle's animated descriptions of Harlem's political and social life, of American imperialism, and of his heroes Marcus Garvey and Frantz Fanon. Bogle was a second-generation New Yorker from Jamaica and grandson of one of Garvey's top assistants. He had left New York for Ghana without, as they say, a pot to piss in or a window to throw it out of. But the brother could wax eloquently about his grandiose plans for Pan-African economic and political development. Bogle was living with a group of Harlem "transnational citizens" who had found work in Accra as teachers, private tutors for Ghanaian elites, clerks in the new US embassy, and low-level entrepreneurs in export/import businesses. Although not segregated from the locals, they had created their own community affectionately called Uhuru, Swahili for "freedom." At first annoyed by Bogle's self-absorption and bravado, over time Joseph got accustomed to his new acquaintance. He found himself spending more and more time with him at the baobab tree.

"When will I get a chance to meet this New York Bogle guy you keep talking about?" Lily asked. "Maybe I'll stop by the baobab and introduce myself."

Joseph had to laugh at the thought. "Lily, you know African culture. Women do not participate in these discussions."

"Well," Lily pressed, "I find it curious that you've never invited him to dinner or to worship with us."

"He's neither a family man nor a churchman."

"Oh," Lily raised an eyebrow. "Then it looks like you have two choices. Either you save him, or you stay away from him."

Joseph knew that there was some truth in what Lily was saying, but he didn't want to deal with it. Instead, he said he was going to take a walk and left.

Although he hadn't planned to go to the tree, Joseph was glad that no one was there when he arrived. He sat down and tried to figure out what was bothering him – and Lily, apparently – about his friendship with Bogle. He was deep in thought when a familiar voice startled him.

"Hey, man," Bogle laughed, "what you doing all alone under the tree. Wife put you out?"

Joseph chuckled and shrugged. "No, brother, I just needed a quiet place to think."

Bogle waved his hand as if to dismiss the idea of thinking and invited Joseph to come home with him to meet his mother and sister who had just arrived from New York. Joseph said he needed to get back home, but Bogle insisted.

"My mom and sister will be in Accra for a few months, and my mom will probably want to come to your church. Come on, Joseph. Besides, you haven't met the other sisters and brothers who live in Uhuru."

Joseph relented. After all, he told himself, it was his pastoral duty to meet newcomers and invite them to his church.

He heard the loud music before he saw the five modest, wood-frame houses with front porches and distinctive African American trademarks – screens on the windows and doors. The houses were built in a semi-circle and shared a common front yard. Fats Domino's *Ain't That a Shame* was blasting from someone's record player.

Bogle swayed side to side. "Don't you just love that Fats Domino?"

"Oh, uh, yeah," Joseph said even though he had no idea who Fats Domino was.

The residents of Uhuru were sitting on their porches or in the common yard chatting softly and listening to music. A billow of smoke emanated from the center of the yard where a small fire, fueled with dried leaves and stalks from the surrounding baobab, coconut, and banana trees, tried but failed to keep the persistent African mosquitoes at bay. Joseph was warmly welcomed with offerings of local palm wine and smuggled Johnny Walker scotch. He accepted a cup of wine. He spent most of his time sitting in the yard talking with Mrs. Bogle, Joseph's mother, who delighted in sharing stories about her storefront church in Bronx, New York's Jamaican community and promised to visit

Joseph's church before she returned to the States. She never mentioned a husband, and Joseph didn't ask. When he got up to leave, Mrs. Bogle insisted he meet her daughter and, in a shrill, voluminous Jamaican patois, called out, "Precious, come! Make haste, girl!"

"Mother, please don't call me that colonial name," Joseph heard someone shout through the dense smoke. "My name is Abena. Can't you remember that? I was born on Tuesday."

"Your name is Precious, last time I looked at your birth certificate," protested Mrs. Bogle.

Joseph stood up to see more clearly just as Abena came out of the house. She was wearing red pedal pushers with an Adinkra cloth wrapped around her waist. The straps of her polka-dot halter top tied behind her neck and her arms and back were bare. Her duku head scarf was elegantly wrapped and flattered her face. Abena made a regal entrance. Joseph couldn't stop staring as she approached him with her right hand extended. He took her hand and grinned like a Cheshire cat.

"Welcome home, Abena."

He was still holding her hand when Bogle stepped forward to formally introduce his younger sister. Abena, he explained, was a recent graduate of the Howard University's College of Fine Arts and a member of the acclaimed Howard Players. After graduation, she had returned to New York to make her mark on Broadway, but after battling rejections – or more to the point, overt racism – Abena had enough. Now, Bogle joked, she knew why Broadway was called *The Great White Way*. He went on to explain that she had decided to remake her image by immersing herself in African dance and music and was thinking of moving to Paris, where her natural eroticism might provide more theatrical opportunities.

Joseph sensed that he was embarrassing himself by staring at Abena. He reiterated that he needed to get home and thanked everyone for welcoming him. But Bogle, apparently agent as well as brother, announced that Abena was working on a new routine and wanted to dance for the group.

"Hold on a minute, my brother. Don't leave yet," he said to Joseph. Then turning to everyone, he said, "I want you folks to check out Abena dancing to a song by New York's next Billie Holiday, Miss Nina Simone singing *My Baby Just Cares for Me*. And now, nurtured on the sweet streets of Harlem and inspired by the spirits of our African ancestors, my sis, Abena Bogle!"

Rid of her head wrap and Akindra waistcloth, Abena danced in her tight pedal pusher pants and revealing halter top. She was a wonderful dancer, making the complicated moves seem effortless. Like African women dancers, she could gyrate her hips and then pulsate up and down while her head and shoulders remained so still that she could have balanced a basket of okra on her head. When she bowed at her waist and spread her arms, she reminded Joseph of the wings of the Phoenix rising from the ashes. She flawlessly integrated Broadway-style high kicks and ballerina pirouettes. Everyone enjoyed the show, but no one enjoyed it more than Abena. She was having fun entertaining herself.

She ended her routine by winking at Joseph and singing the last verse of the song with Nina.

Nina's sultry voice and Abena's enticing body had filled Joseph with a lust so intense it felt like an out-of-body experience. Unfortunately, his head was not the only part of his body that was reacting to her performance, and he felt unbearable shame as he shifted the cap on his lap. Since he couldn't stand up without embarrassing himself, he asked for another glass of palm wine, praying his body would not reveal where his mind had been. It took another glass of wine before he could get up to stagger home.

Lily was waiting, visibly upset. "Where you been, Joseph Washington? It's midnight! I didn't know if you were dead or alive."

"Oh, sorry. I didn't realize it was so late. Ran into Bogle, and he wanted to introduce me to his mother, who is visiting for a while. She's doing lots of good missionary work with the Jamaican population in New York."

"Talking about church stuff, huh? Well, you're obviously drunk and you smell like a nightclub! We've been married for thirteen years, and I've *never* seen you behave like this. I don't know what you and that Bogle guy are up to, but it can't be good!"

Lily wanted to scream at him, but she thought about Neema and Aunt Eni and instead stomped off to their bedroom. Joseph watched as his wife angrily closed the bedroom door. Sitting on the sofa listening to his wife sob throughout the night, he vowed that he would never again hurt the love of his life.

The next few weeks, Joseph tried to resume his work and repair his marriage. He stopped going to the baobab tree and instead stayed home with Lily and Neema. He aimlessly planned one project after another – a building fund campaign, a traveling gospel quartet, and a women's sewing cooperative – but he couldn't really focus and so none of his plans saw the light of day. He was in constant motion, as if a quiet moment would remind him of how much he missed the baobab group, his friendship with Bogle, and, as guilty as he felt admitting it, seeing Abena. She was not an intellectually interesting or even mature person, but that didn't matter to him. Joseph was enthralled with the way her body moved when she danced – her pulsating hips, the bounce of her firm breasts, her outstretched arms that seemed to invite him to come closer. Images of Abena haunted him.

Lily was a well-respected educator and organizer in Accra and had risen in the ranks of women's church and civic groups. A couple of months after Joseph's drunken night at Uhuru, Lily traveled to Cape Coast to participate in a three-day interdenominational women's missionary meeting. Joseph was determined to stay busy while she was gone, so he volunteered to preach at the evening revival service of Changed Life Baptist Church, a well-known church pastured by Rev. Essien in a neighboring district. Rev. Essien himself came to pick up Joseph. As he and Joseph were walking to the car, he said there was another rider who had expressed an interest in attending the revival. To Joseph's surprise, they drove to Uhuru and out came Mrs. Bogle and Abena.

"What a pleasant surprise," Abena laughed.

"How are you, Mrs. Bogle? Abena?" Joseph tried to direct his attention to the mother.

"Much better now," said Abena, "much better. Maybe I'll see you when the reverend brings Mother home," she purred.

It was the worst sermon that Joseph had ever preached. The Accra Baptists were a polite and encouraging group, but even their lukewarm "Preach, Brother, preach!" couldn't bring the Holy Ghost to the pulpit. The congregants left the revival convinced that their long-held belief was accurate: Methodists can't preach.

On the way back to take Mrs. Bogle home, Rev. Essien stopped short of the front yard of Uhuru and parked his car on an adjacent dusty road behind a row of bushes. Joseph wondered why the reverend had parked in such an out of the way spot until Rev. Essien turned to give him a wink and said, "Be back in a minute. Gotta see this nice lady to her door."

Joseph was angry. As if things weren't bad enough, now he was complicit in some sleazy business going on between Rev. Essien and Mrs. Bogle. After twenty minutes sitting and stewing in the car's backseat, Joseph opened the door to go looking for the missing preacher. Before his foot hit the dirt, he heard her voice.

"Hey, Joseph, Rev. Essien wanted me to tell you that he'll be ready to leave in a few minutes."

Joseph looked and saw Abena's smooth brown face, softly illuminated by the moonlight, coming closer and closer. She was hypnotic, like a mythological siren that no man could resist. Joseph wasn't quite sure how or when she slid into the backseat beside him, but every nerve in his body came alive when she placed her hand on what she wanted. And even as his head told him he shouldn't, his body couldn't resist. He'd never made love to a woman who took charge, and it was spine-tingling. She choreographed their moves like one of her dance performances. Her moans and requests were loud. She was unapologetic about her pleasure. Abena didn't so much leave after they finished lovemaking as she just evaporated into the fog of the steamy Ghanaian night.

Before Joseph could absorb the magnitude of his heinous sin, Rev. Essien crept around the bushes and jumped into his car like a petty thief in the night. Joseph had been used, played, as they say, by two deceitful characters. One was the unscrupulous married preacher who needed Joseph to cover his sexual pursuit of Mrs. Bogle, and the other was Abena, the reckless young woman who needed Joseph to satisfy her sexual desires. Joseph couldn't expose Abena as a loose woman because he was a married man and a preacher. And Joseph couldn't expose Rev. Essien as an adulterer because so was he! Joseph wanted to cry. He had been duped into an immoral sexual drama. Joseph was the only one in the game who didn't have an ace up his sleeve. He was the perfect pawn.

The next morning Aunt Eni didn't speak to him. Fortunately, Neema's constant chatter covered the awkward silence, but Eni's nonverbal behavior let Joseph know that she had heard him come home last night and that she knew that revival meetings end much earlier. Joseph felt panicky. One thing was for sure in Africa. There were no secrets. Many times, he had heard African men joke about extramarital affairs by reminding each other that bushes have ears and walls have eyes. He gave Neema a quick goodbye kiss on her forehead and rushed out of the kitchen without finishing his breakfast. He only had a few hours to get himself together before picking up Lily at the Coach bus terminal in downtown Accra.

That night Joseph confessed his sin to Lily. He avoided the details and chose his words carefully, hoping to spare Lily the pain of an overly descriptive *mea culpa*. It probably didn't matter. She understood that "not being forthcoming" was lying, that "not thinking straight" meant drunk, that "impure thoughts" was lust, and that an "inappropriate relationship" meant sex.

"Lily, I'm not making any excuses, but now I can see that losing Kwame had a more profound effect on me than I realized. I thought I could be the husband and father who could mend his broken family, but I never really worked on mending what was broken in me. I have failed miserably. Please, Lily, I've asked God and now I'm asking you. Please, please forgive me."

Lily stared at him belligerently. "How dare you use Kwame's death as an excuse for your despicable, shameful behavior. I don't care about and don't want to hear about your pain!" Her eyes narrowed. "Forgive you? You lied from the very beginning, conveniently not telling me that Bogle's sister was traveling with his mother. But I met her before you did. Was introduced to her at the market. Old folks got it right – God does work in mysterious ways. Abena's a Jezebel, and you're just a dumb ass. Let me tell you something you should never forget, Joseph Washington. You're *way* out of your league. Pope City boy, who just fell off the turnip truck, this New York hussy doesn't want you. That Howard University hussy from New York can have her pick of the litter. She certainly doesn't want a country boy like you from Pope City, Georgia."

"Lily, please, I don't want her," he begged. "It wasn't even about her, really. It was just all this pent-up emotion from losing Kwame. Please, this is not who I am. I want to be with you. Forever. Please, forgive me."

Lily was unmoved. "I'll get back to you on that. Just remember – I am not like my mother, who took whatever life dished out to her. She sucked it up and made lemonade out of lemons. When life peed on her, she just called it rain. Well, not *me*, Joseph Washington." She waved her hand as if to dismiss her husband. "I'll get back to you."

The days dragged by for Joseph. Lily wasn't aggressive or unresponsive like Aunt Eni, who still wasn't talking to him. Instead, Lily answered Joseph's questions about household or church matters and put up a good front for friends and parishioners. She went about her regular duties constantly singing *Amazing Grace*. Joseph thought he would lose his mind.

Putting up a cheerful front for Neema turned out to be more difficult, however. Always sensitive to her surroundings, Neema noticed the change in the adults in the house. She used to enjoy watching her father sneak up to grab her mother around the waist and whisper in her ear. Neema would giggle and have fun repeating her mother's playful response: "Joseph, you're so silly." But little lighthearted exchanges like this weren't happening anymore. Confused, she would try to fix things.

"Mother, grab Daddy's hand and let's play London Bridge Is Falling Down."

"Aunt Eni," she'd prompt, "tell Daddy about the policeman who was chasing that boy in the market today."

Finally, Lily told Joseph that she was ready to talk. She explained that when she was at the Cape Coast church conference, she met Mrs. Hudson, the wife of the president of Fisk University. Mrs. Hudson had heard about Lily's work as a teacher and organizer and had been anxious to meet her. It also didn't hurt that Lily was a Fisk alum, as were her parents, and a former member of the university's famed Jubilee Singers. Mrs. Hudson told Lily that she had seen her presentation to the AME Bishop and Presiding Elders and thought it was outstanding. She also reported that one of Lily's church members had said she was a great communicator who could speak with anyone, from African dignitaries to illiterate village women. Mrs. Hudson had even given her a lighthearted compliment, saying "I have to take my hat off to any woman who can get us Negro church ladies to start on time and stick with a plan." Lily was flattered but didn't expect what came next. Mrs. Hudson offered her a job at Fisk. Apparently, her husband was looking for a "cultured and cosmopolitan" executive administrative assistant who understood the Fisk culture but who was not so provincial as to be frightened by new possibilities. She thought Lily would be perfect, although she realized that Lily might not available until Joseph's church assignment in Africa ended.

"Joseph, I've decided to accept the position. I told Mrs. Hudson that I was returning to the States sooner than expected to be closer to my aging parents."

Joseph was devastated, but all he could think to say was, "Lily, how could you make up a lie like that?"

"Really, Joseph?" she said sarcastically. "Do you really want to talk about lying?"

Joseph hung his head.

"Aunt Alfreda has wired me the airfare," she continued, "and Neema and I are leaving next month." Joseph tried to interrupt but Lily put up her hand to stop him. "The Fisk offer is generous. We can live rent-free in an apartment in the dorm where I will be on-call as the night dorm mother. Neema can attend the university's elementary laboratory school for free, and Mrs. Hudson has assured me that the campus is full of young Christian women who could babysit Neema in the evenings if I am needed at work."

Lily had made up her mind and refused to hear any of Joseph's objections.

On July 4, 1958, Lily and nine-year-old Neema left Accra. The departure was heart-wrenching. Neema screamed for her Daddy and Aunt Eni. Joseph tried to calm her with promises.

"Don't worry, Sweetie. Before you know it, Daddy will join you and your mother. I've just got to wrap up some church business first. You'll see. I'll be there in no time."

As his family climbed the steep steps to the plane, a grief-stricken Joseph looked stone-faced in the distance. He wanted to cry, but no tears would flow. Aunt Eni was waving goodbye and wailing like she was at a funeral, but no one took notice because that's how Ghanaians said goodbye.

The long flight seemed like a ride in an endless dark tunnel. Trapped in the crowded plane with Neema squeezing her arm between restless fits of sleep and tears, Lily wondered how her life and thirteen-year marriage could unravel so quickly.

Once they had become attuned to the rhythm of life in Nashville, which was undeniably less colorful and exciting than Accra, Lily and Neema settled into their new routine on Fisk's campus. Lily and Joseph communicated often by mail, and Joseph and Neema wrote to each other as well. Lily put up a good front trying to make the best of a bad situation. Neema missed her father and Aunt Eni terribly. She was also mad at her mother for taking her away from them. Lily and Neema were in constant conflict about matters large and small.

Without Eni's help on school mornings, Lily tried to establish new routines with Neema.

"Guess what we're having for breakfast? Corn flakes and a banana! This is what I ate when I was growing up in Little Rock. It's yummy!"

Neema watched suspiciously as her mother shook the dry flakes into a bowl, poured milk on them, and then placed slices of bananas around the edges of the bowl.

"Neema, isn't that cute? Try it. I guarantee you're going to love it."

Neema slowly put a spoonful in her mouth and gagged.

"Yuck! It tastes like straw! I want Aunt Eni! She used to fix me plantains and *fufu* for breakfast."

Lily tried to lift Neema's spirits by taking her to places she'd never seen before, like Nashville's large department stores with their ruffled dresses, petticoats, patent leather shoes, and socks with lace trim. She also occasionally took Neema on trips that she chaperoned for Fisk women, places like Atlanta, Memphis, and Mobile. Neema had fun on these outings, but Lily knew that her daughter's life was incomplete without her father.

For Neema's tenth birthday, Lily had a big surprise. The university's president, Dr. Hudson, had arranged a transatlantic call to Joseph. When Lily told Neema that she would be talking to her father on the telephone, Neema responded with a joyous ululation that Aunt Eni had taught her when she was a toddler. Lily hadn't heard the high-pitched shrilling sound since they had left Ghana. Neema gave her mother the biggest kiss on the cheek that she had given her in a long time. Neema was excited and she ran ahead of Lily to Dr. Hudson's office. When the connection finally came through, Neema couldn't stand still.

"I'm first," she kept repeating as she jumped up and down. "Me first!" Lily laughed as she handed her the receiver.

"Hi, Daddy. I love you. You should see my new bedroom! When are you coming to live with us?"

"I'm working on it, Baby Girl. I—"

Neema interrupted. "Daddy, that's what you always say in your letters. But when are you coming home? When? I miss you."

Joseph changed the subject by telling her that Aunt Eni said to tell her *Mafe wo*, I've missed you. He asked about her school and told her how proud he was of her good grades.

"Neema," Lily whispered, "remember we agreed that we can only talk for a few minutes. Tell your father goodbye and go wait on the steps. I'll be out in a minute."

Lily had not heard Joseph's voice in a year. He wrote long letters to her and Neema, so there was no need to waste time on unnecessary chatter. Instead, he again asked for her forgiveness and to allow him to come live with her and Neema. Lily listened to his baritone voice and thought about how much she missed him. Truth be told, she longed to have him hold her close.

"I have to go, Joseph. Dr. Hudson has already been so generous."

"Okay, sweetheart, but please think about us living together again. I love you and need you and Neema with me."

"I need you, too," Lily admitted.

The telephone call was not the first time that Lily missed having Joseph by her side. Every day on Fisk's campus was a constant reminder of their love. She was the dorm mother in the same building she had been living in when she met Joseph. All the university's major events were held in the chapel where they married. The Fisk Jubilee Choir sang at most assemblies and the program invariably included *Steal Away*. And there were the more intimate reminders. She couldn't enter Carnegie Library without thinking about the first time he kissed her behind the stacks.

Lily spent many restless nights thinking about what she should do. Did she want to reconcile her marriage just to have a man? Was she capable of forgiveness? Could her love for him ever be the same? Was Neema's well-being enough of a reason to allow Joseph to return? Although she never really stopped struggling with these issues, in the end she decided that it was time for her family to be whole again.

Joseph came to Nashville to live in December of 1959, and it was the best Christmas gift Neema could have received. The family moved into a rental home not far from campus. At first, Neema would follow Joseph around the house, and, when he left, she would panic. "Where are you going, Daddy. When are you coming back? Can I go with you?" Both Joseph and Lily were worried that Neema might have developed abandonment issues.

The Washingtons eventually purchased their own home with money they had saved and lived a comfortable, middle-class life. For the most part, their life was centered within Nashville's all-Black communities – the AME church and the neighborhoods where many Fisk, Tennessee State, and Meharry Medical College professionals resided.

Joseph had made the best of his year alone in Accra and arrived in Nashville with a newly earned Master of Divinity degree from the University of Accra and a license to minister in the AME church. The bishop, who was aware of Joseph's indiscretion, hesitantly assigned him as assistant pastor in one of Nashville's largest congregations, Ebenezer AME. Joseph understood that the bishop was disappointed, not because he had committed adultery, but because he got caught with an unsaved woman who didn't know, or refused to follow, the rules of the game. More incriminating, his wife had left him and returned to the States. The bishop prayed that Joseph had learned some hard lessons and could be trusted with his pastoral duties.

A few months after Joseph arrived, the Fisk campus that he and Lily knew as students started to change. Like on campuses throughout the country, a new consciousness was spreading among the Black students at Fisk. In March of 1960, ten students showed up at Lily's desk.

"We want to speak to President Hudson immediately!"

As the president's executive assistant, Lily Washington was a skilled gatekeeper. A bit annoyed by the student's demanding voice and bad manners, Lily calmly asked, "Do you have an appointment?"

"No, we don't, but he needs to understand what's getting ready to go down here," the apparent leader shouted.

"Young man, who do you think you're talking to? I suggest that all of you leave right now. Select one person to come back tomorrow and I'll see if there's any room on Dr. Hudson's calendar in the next couple of days. Now, in a few words, tell me the purpose of the meeting."

"Mrs. Washington," the leader said, reading her nameplate, "what we have to say can't be reduced to a few words. We'll leave. Dr. Hudson can read about it in tomorrow's newspaper."

The following morning the entire city read the headline in the *Nashville Tennessean*: "Negro College Students Jailed During Sit-ins." The Black Nationalist Movement had officially begun in Nashville. Joseph was pleasantly surprised and excited about what it might mean for the city.

As assistant pastor, Joseph performed all the duties that the senior pastor loathed. He conducted Wednesday night Bible study, visited the sick and shut-in, directed Sunday school and vacation Bible school, presided over funerals for "less important" church members, christened screaming babies, and preached at the 8:00 a.m. Sunday service. Joseph found his assignments mundane and uninspiring, but he never complained.

In a sad twist, Joseph's ministry changed for the better when the senior pastor died unexpectedly. Joseph had developed strong connections with many members of the church as well as with some key community leaders, and they lobbied the bishop to promote Joseph to the senior position. As soon as he was installed, he began to align Ebenezer AME with the new Black activist liberation theology. He broadened the congregation by recruiting members from housing projects and from the African and Caribbean students attending the local colleges. He accepted invitations to sit on the governing boards of the local NAACP, Black YMCA, and Nashville General Hospital. He started a childcare center in the basement of the church and opened the church's kitchen during holidays and semester breaks to feed foreign college students who couldn't go back home to visit their families. Soon there were no empty pews on Sundays. Hearing of its success, Martin Luther King, Jr. selected Ebenezer AME for a civil rights rally when the Negro community boycotted Nashville's downtown stores.

With their careers taking off, Joseph and Lily worked hard to resolve their marital issues and settled into a comfortable, albeit not necessarily passionate, relationship. By the time Neema was a teenager, she had concluded that public kissing, hugging, holding hands, and saying "I love you" were definitely things that only happened in white Hollywood movies. She never saw her parents behave that way. She saw other positive signs, however, that relieved some of her anxieties about her parents' marriage.

One day after school, Neema noticed two copies of a book she hadn't seen before, *Go Tell It on the Mountain* by James Baldwin. "Whose books are these, Mother?" she asked.

"Oh, just a book your father and are going to read. It's about a teenaged preacher and his family in New York City. Think we're going to enjoy it. Can't wait to discuss it with your father!"

Lily and Joseph were laughing together more often, visiting friends, and enjoying their alone time with each other. Lily even decided to join Ebenezer's choir and renew her interest in music and singing.

One Sunday, Joseph finished reading the Biblical texts and was about to begin his sermon when he had a spontaneous thought.

"Church, I have been inspired to ask the choir to bear with me. If it pleases the Church, I would like my wife to come down from the choir stand and help me sing our favorite hymn, *Steal Away*."

The congregation was delighted and people stood up to give their consent with spirited applause and shouts of "Amen." Little did they know that this was the spiritual that had brought them together.

Lily and Joseph also started attending many of Nashville's social events – anniversary celebrations, birthday parties, and NAACP and Greek fundraising dances. Neema decided her parents needed to learn the new dance craze, The Twist, and soon dancing to music on the local Black radio station became one of the family's favorite activities. Sometimes, Lily and Joseph slow danced together. "My turn, Daddy, Neema would suggest as she tapped on his back, but most of the time Joseph ignored her.

When she was twelve years old, Neema woke up one morning with bloodstains in her panties.

"Daddy, Mother, help! I'm sick."

"What's wrong, Baby Girl," Joseph asked as he and Lily rushed into their daughter's room.

"My panties have blood in them, and my stomach hurts. What's wrong with me?"

"Oh! Uh . . ." Joseph turned to his wife. "You got this, right?"

Lily smiled at her husband's discomfort. "Go," she said as she shooed him away with her hands. "We'll be fine."

Neema had no idea what was going on.

"Go wash up real good. I'll bring you a pad and show you how to use it to soak up the blood. Then

I'll get you some pills and a hot water bottle for the cramps. No school today."

Lily returned with a blue cardboard box decorated with a picture of a large white rose. The word Kotex was printed in large letters. Lily pulled out a thick, ten-inch-long cotton pad that had a four-inch strip of fabric at each end. She slipped each end of the pad into one of two hooks hanging from a thin elastic waistband.

"Put this on," she instructed. "I'll help you."

When Neema was settled back in bed with the uncomfortable pad between her legs and the red rubber hot water bottle on her stomach, Lily handed her a booklet entitled, *You're a Young Lady Now.* Neema wasn't as scared as she had been earlier, but she was still very confused.

"Neema, baby, you've started your period, which is another word for menstruation. I know you're afraid because of the blood, but every female on earth menstruates every month. The fact that you're doing it just means that you're growing up, so don't be afraid. I want you to read this booklet, and we'll discuss it later."

The hot water bottle was steadily easing her cramps. With nothing better to do, Neema started reading the booklet.

Blood and other fluids leave your body once a month over a period of 3-7 days. The blood comes from an organ in your body called the womb, and when you get married and have a baby, this is where the baby grows.

Neema didn't understand most of what she read, but she decided then and there that she would never have a baby.

Before her second period arrived, Neema and her mother had talked a few times about menstruation, but Neema still couldn't make sense of what her mother was saying. She showed Neema a picture of a smiling white couple in bed with blankets pulled up to their necks. A barely visible smiling baby was nestled between them. Lily recognized her daughter's lack of understanding and decided to cut to the chase.

"Neema, you are a young woman now and a very pretty one. Just like your body is changing, boys are going through some changes as well. They will start noticing you and want to be close to you, have sex with you. Listen to me." Lily's tone became stern. "Don't *ever*," she repeated, "*ever* let a boy touch your private parts. Only married people have sex to express their love. If you don't remember anything else from this book, remember that now you can have a baby. And if you're not married, a baby will ruin your life *forever*. Do you have any questions?"

The harshness of her mother's tone left Neema so completely flustered that the only response she could muster was, "Maybe later." Neema never asked her mother anything else about menstruation or sex. "What is Mother talking about? Blood coming between your legs. Boys touch you down there. You have a baby and your life is ruined!"

Neema tried to visualize exactly what sex was but couldn't. What were her parents doing in bed? Neema finally put the whole issue to rest by concluding that whatever sex was, it obviously meant that her parents loved each other. Her mother and the book said so. However, she was also pretty sure that they had had sex only twice, once to produce her and again for Baby Kwame.

Even though Joseph had joined his family in Nashville, Neema still felt a void in her life. She missed Aunt Eni terribly. She could still hear her nagging call – "N-e-e-e-ma, come!" She missed how Eni would smell like the garlic and ginger and other spices she cooked with, her high-pitched laugh, and those daily grooming rituals like greasing Neema's knees with shea butter and braiding her thick hair. Neema vowed that one day she would return to Accra and find her Aunt Eni.

Neema had always done well at Fisk Elementary Laboratory School, but she blossomed after Joseph's return. During the weekdays at Fisk, she was Lily Washington's precocious child whom everyone knew and loved. The campus was her playground. On Sundays, she was the preacher's kid who could steal the show at every church event, from Emancipation Day Service on January 1 to Watch Night Prayer Meeting on December 31. Things changed when she enrolled at the public high school. She didn't know any of the other students, and she didn't fit in with any of the social groups – not the cheerleaders or band kids or the nerds or athletes, and certainly not with girls who had boyfriends.

By the time she was thirteen, Neema had the look of the typical homecoming queen or majorette: nicely proportioned body, shapely legs, long, wavy hair, and skin the color of which Lily said she had inherited from her light-complexioned maternal grandmother. Several of the boys in her high school thought she was cute and sought her help with their homework and school projects, but no one asked her for a date. The general opinion was that she talked too much, read too much, asked too many questions, and challenged too many authority figures. In a word, she was trouble. Girls whispered that she was stuck up and thought she was better than everybody else. Neema tried not to let the gossip bother her.

Despite Lily's urging, she refused to join Jack and Jill, an exclusive social club for the children of upper middle-class Black families, and she cried for days when Lily insisted that she participate in the Black community's Debutante Ball.

Joseph's office was Neema's hideaway, the refuge where she could share her adolescent angst and secrets. Neema told her father, and never her mother, about boys she had crushes on and girls who teased and bullied her. Because her father was such a source of comfort and advice for her, Neema didn't understand why her mother picked on him so much. Like Neema, it seemed that Joseph could never please Lily. But unlike his daughter, Joseph never complained about or resisted Lily.

Neema didn't know why, but Accra was a taboo subject. Whenever she tried to recall the details of a pleasant memory or favorite landmark, neither Lily nor Joseph seemed to want to talk about it. As she got older, she figured that something terrible must have happened there. Still, she had loved living in Accra and wanted to see it again. When she was younger, she once asked Joseph if the two of them could leave her mother in Nashville and go to Accra together. Joseph's response was quick and emphatic.

"Baby Girl, I love you, but I also love your mother and will never leave her behind." He hugged Neema, grabbed her hand, and smiled. "Now let's go get our weekly ice cream cone from Dairy Queen. Don't forget to ask your mother to come with us." Lily never went with them.

CHAPTER FOUR

ACCRA, GHANA
WASHINGTON, DC

Two months after she graduated from Howard University in 1970, Neema left Dulles Airport outside of DC headed for Accra, Ghana as a Peace Corps volunteer. All the memories of the first eight years of her life there were happy ones, and she desperately wanted to hold on to them.

Neema's first few weeks of Peace Corps orientation in Ghana were uninspiring but tolerable. Neema and Vincent, who was a graduate of another historically Black college, were the only Black volunteers in the group of thirty, and they suffered through some ignorant and insulting questions posed by the other group members: Why are our African guides always late? Why does everybody talk so fast? Is it safe to walk by yourself at night? Neema wondered whether they had learned *anything* before arriving. The instructor knew that Neema was born in Accra and spent eight years there with her missionary parents, but he never asked about her experiences or mentioned the fact to her fellow volunteers. Neema didn't care. She didn't want the group to start asking her silly questions and relying on her for survival. So, she kept quiet and hoped that what the other volunteers lacked in cultural experience and information, they compensated with enthusiasm and commitment.

Neema focused on her goals for this new adventure: find Aunt Eni, revisit some of her favorite places, forget Nigel, and figure out the rest of her life. The first free Sunday that the volunteers had away from the overly protective Peace Corps supervisor, Neema purchased some flowers, boarded an overcrowded *tro tro* bus, and headed to her father's old church to visit her brother's grave. She was also hoping that Aunt Eni would be there. She had ridden these *tro tros* as a child and realized that she still enjoyed the discordant mix of people, crops, shop wares, and crates of chickens.

Neema exited the bus and was shocked to see that the parsonage where her family had lived was gone. The vacant lot showed no trace that a house had ever stood there. She knew her parents would be heartbroken when she told them. Otherwise, not much else had changed about Turner Mission AME in twelve years. The outdoor church sign read, *Sunday Service, 11:00 am. Welcome. Rev. Kwesi Boateng.* Neema was early, so she took the opportunity to walk around the building. The ornate, hand-carved, double wooden doors that had been installed during her father's ministry stood in stark contrast to the rest of the unassuming building. The warped and cracked aluminum siding needed a paint job. The five concrete steps leading to the entrance were chipped and had hairline cracks. The over-sized wooden cross that once sat on top of the louvered bell tower was gone. Probably lost in a hurricane, Neema thought.

Neema peeped in the windows and saw that the hand-carved benches had been replaced with pews with backs. The picture of the white Jesus that her father replaced with a dove on top of a cross had returned as the centerpiece on the back wall. The small choir loft behind the altar still accommodated the scratched, probably still out-of-tune piano.

When Neema went to the cemetery behind the church, she was relieved to see that it was being well maintained. Not remembering the exact place where Kwame was buried, she walked over the entire cemetery searching for her brother's plot. The hodgepodge of graves included traditional grave markers sitting on slabs along with crudely made wooden crosses with the names of the deceased scribbled on them. There were also grave markers that Neema remembered from her childhood – rocks, seashells, and cracked pottery arranged in interesting patterns. Finally, she came upon Kwame's grave.

Kwame Joseph Washington
March 30, 1955 – May 27, 1955
An Angel Forever Loved

Neema was surprised by the slow trickle of tears that dampened her cheeks. She cleaned the grave marker and placed her small bouquet of flowers on top. She took pictures to send to her parents. They would be both sad and pleased.

When no one had arrived at the church by 10:45, Neema decided to walk around. A lot of the structures she remembered were gone, but the pungent smell of mackerel being smoked in oil-burning drums and the rhythmic thuds of women pounding cassava were the same. The one thing that she was sure hadn't changed was the baobab tree. She found it easily. As soon as she saw the tree, she remembered sitting here with her father as he told her stories about his boyhood in Pope City, Georgia. Even though it was an impossible task, Neema never left the tree without trying to climb it. She invariably failed, but her father always encouraged her: "Keep trying, Neema. One day you're going to climb that tree!"

Neema sat on the ground facing the tree's massive trunk, assumed a yoga pose, closed her eyes, and thought about all the happy times she had had in Accra, like when she helped her mother teach women to read, or when her father taught her to ride a bicycle, or Aunt Eni chatting happily as she braided Neema's hair. When Neema opened her eyes, she was startled to see a small group of children standing in the road bewildered. They were accustomed to seeing vanloads of foreign tourists in the neighborhood, but this woman was squatting by herself with no van or car in sight. Neema greeted them in Akan, but they didn't speak back. She was sure the children were going to run back home to tell their mothers that they had seen a spirit or maybe just some crazy Black American lady who had missed her tour bus.

Neema looked at her watch and realized she was late for church. When she was within earshot, she heard the pitiful singing of the congregation. There were only a few dozen members so there was no way to sneak into the church. She opened the creaky door, and the whole congregation turned around. The sole usher, dressed in all white uniform and a nurse's cap, gave Neema a blurred mimeographed copy of the order of service. Neema took a seat on the back pew and listened as Rev. Boateng delivered an overly dramatic sermon. He was what her mother would call "a whooping and hollering jackleg preacher."

"I don't think you folks hear me?" he intoned. "Let me say that one more time. Can I get a witness? Help me out, Church." The compliant church members responded with a few predictable *Amens* and *Preach, Reverend*.

Rev. Boateng could not ignore the unfamiliar visitor with a huge Afro and oversized hoop earrings or how her entrance had distracted his congregation.

"Church, the Lord has blessed us with a visitor this morning," he said, stretching his arm in Neema's direction. "Let the Church say Amen. Miss, please stand up and bring greetings in any way the spirit moves you."

Neema was a preacher's kid and so she knew exactly what to say and how to say it.

"First, give honor and glory to God. Pastor Boateng, members of the Trustee Board, and my Turner

Mission family, my name is Neema Washington, and I am the daughter of your former pastor, Rev. Joseph Washington, and Mrs. Lily Washington. They named me after their favorite hymn, *Amazing Grace*. I bring you greetings from both. I am so thrilled to be home. I was born here and christened in this church. Some of you may even remember me. I spent the first eight years of my life here."

There was quiet murmuring among the church members. A few had gasped when she called her father's name, while others had stood up and shouted, "Praise the Lord!" When Aunt Eni did not come running down the aisle, Neema knew she was not there. Trying not to show her disappointment, she continued.

"My parents are blessed and in good health in America. My father is pastor of Ebenezer AME Church in Nashville, Tennessee. My mother, Lily, works in the office of a college president. I am here in Accra with the Peace Corps to continue the same kind of work my parents started here. Pray for me as I seek the Lord's guidance in this next phase of my life."

When she had finished speaking, the congregation spontaneously burst into a joyous welcome. Many remembered Neema. Women with oversized breasts nearly smothered her with hugs. Men wouldn't stop shaking her hand. She wanted to ask about Aunt Eni, but she didn't want to interrupt the celebration. One elderly woman with a cane, whose face she recognized but name she couldn't remember, stood alone leaning on one of the pews. She finally got her chance to speak to Neema.

"Hope you remember me," she said softly. "My name is Yaa Awuku. Sometimes I helped your Aunt Eni take care of you in the market. She and your mother taught me how to read. I'm so thankful for what your mother did for me. It changed my life!"

Neema put her hand on top of the woman's in a gesture of appreciation for her words.

"I am one of the oldest members of this church and was here the first Sunday your father preached in this pulpit. Since you said you just arrived, I guess you don't know. Your Aunt Eni passed away last year."

Neema slumped on the pew in front of Yaa Awuku and buried her face in her hands.

"I'm so sorry you didn't get a chance to see her. She would be happy to know what a beautiful woman you've become."

People gathered around Neema and comforted her as she cried. She composed herself and remained until the end of the service, although she wasn't really listening to Rev. Boateng. Instead, she thought about all the Christmas and Easter speeches she had recited, songs she had sung, and Bible verses she had read as a child in this church. She could visualize her mother sitting beside her in the front row as they watched her handsome, eloquent father preaching in the pulpit. She could see Baby Kwame's small, bassinette-shaped coffin sitting in front of the altar. Neema breathed deeply to avoid feeling overcome with sadness.

On Sunday mornings, her mother's passive role as the pastor's wife was in stark contrast to her behind-the-scenes work during the week. Neema wondered if the church members ever understood how hard Lily worked. In addition to her full-time teaching job, she organized the reading clinic, trained the communion Sunday stewards, taught the AME discipline and doctrines to the leadership teams, prepared the quarterly and annual reports, and kept the financial ledgers.

Neema's attention returned to the church service when she heard Rev. Boateng reference the scripture about tithing and the poor widow lady who had only two coins and gave one to the church. Neema reached in her purse and put a five-dollar bill in the usher's basket.

There's one last thing, Neema thought. Opening the doors of the Church, and then I'm out of here! The Reverend laid it on heavy. "The Lord's telling me that there's someone in this sanctified place that's a long way from home and who needs a spiritual family."

That was not subtle, Neema thought. I'll just wait him out. Finally, when Neema did not come forward to join the Church, Rev. Boateng gave up and rendered the benediction.

The last part of the service took place outside. The congregants filed out the church building and reconvened in the front yard for the fifteen-minute goodbye ritual. The same people who had been so welcoming to her inside the church did the same outside. Rev. Boateng, broadly grinning, pulled her aside.

"Young lady, I am so grateful that you blessed us with your presence this morning. I hope you come back and bring all your friends from the Peace Corps with you."

Apparently, the reverend had noticed the US five-dollar bill that Neema had put in the offering basket, the equivalent of two months' salary for the average Ghanaian.

Neema made her way through the well-wishers and started walking to the bus station when she heard a woman's voice call her name.

"Neema, wait." It was Mrs. Awuku. "I have to tell you something. You need to know what happened to Eni after your father left the country. She would want you to know."

They found a shady spot out of the way of the heavy pedestrian traffic to talk.

"Ah," Mrs. Awuku sighed, "Eni loved you like you were her own. She worked for a few years in the home of another minister but left that job when she married a widower with four children. Her new husband was not a Christian man and treated her poorly. I never said this to Eni, but I believe the man married her because he knew that she had saved lots of the money from working for your family." Mrs. Awuku shook her head sadly. "Well, the next thing I see is the husband building a new house and moving in his sick mother and two of his sisters' families. Neema, after that, Eni couldn't leave the house because she had to care for her mother-in-law and all those children while everybody was working. She came to church if she could get away, but she always looked so sad. She died last year. Wasn't sick, just passed away in the middle of the night. The Turner Mission family gave her a nice funeral and joyous send-off. She's buried behind the church."

Neema was saddened to hear that her Aunt Eni's life had been so hard. She asked Mrs. Awuku to show her Eni's grave, and they walked to a mound of dirt decorated with stones placed in the shape of a cross. Neema wiped tears from her eyes and took some of the flowers off Kwame's grave and placed them on Eni's.

"Mrs. Awuku, thank you so much for telling me about Aunt Eni. Her life was a difficult one, but I needed to know what happened to her. I will get a proper grave marker for her."

Neema followed through on her promise and purchased an impressive headstone for Eni. She never attended church services at Turner Mission again, but she visited the graves of her two lost loved ones often.

It took Neema a month to re-evaluate what she wanted to accomplish while in Accra after her visit to Turner AME. She overhauled her agenda to be less about goals and more about "going with the flow." She was questioning why she was always so focused on accomplishing something and wanted to experiment with new ways of envisioning her future. She was ready to venture into uncharted waters. She titled her new approach "Making Up for Lost Time" and posted the slogan on the wall over her bed.

Her first project was Vincent, the other Black Peace Corps volunteer. He was a recent graduate of historically Black Trinity College in Georgia. It was a small, Seventh Day Adventist school and the antithesis of Howard. The students at Trinity hailed from rural or small southern towns and were deeply religious and conservative in all aspects of their lives. They abstained from alcohol, smoking, coffee, soft drinks, red meat, dancing, and pre-marital sex. Everyone on Trinity's campus observed a twenty-four-hour Sabbath from sunset on Friday until sunset on Saturday. Vincent was a reluctant Peace Corps volunteer who had been cajoled by his white mentor into pursuing a career as an Adventist missionary. His fiancée was expected to join him in Ghana after she graduated. Despite knowing all this, Neema had decided that Vincent might be a good substitute for Nigel. While he lacked Nigel's intellectual heft, worldly exposure, political consciousness, and charm, he met the primary qualification. Vincent was a sexual neophyte who wouldn't recognize that she was as well.

It didn't take much for Neema to get Vincent's interest. She made excuses for them to spend time together and, when they were alone, she put on a worldly attitude that suggested she was an erotic *femme fatale* who could teach Vincent a thing or two about pleasure. Her acting was straight out of some cheesy B-movie. When Vincent eventually succumbed to his basic instincts and pulled her close, Neema couldn't put the image of her and Nigel making love out of her mind. She fought back tears and realized that her "project" had been a mistake. Flustered and ashamed, she told Vincent that she was sorry for leading him on but they could only be friends, not lovers.

Neema figured out another script to quickly end the affair. "Vincent, the time we spent together the other night was wrong. You are engaged, and I feel so guilty and ashamed. We can still be friends but certainly not lovers."

Vincent was buying it. "Neema, it's OK. I prayed and asked for forgiveness. Tried to set things right with God, myself, and my fiancée. I see a future with you."

Neema was sad and speechless. Her "Making Up for Lost Time" plan had backfired. Vincent was devastated, ashamed, and kept to himself for the remaining months of that first year. Finally, he went home for the summer break, a defeated man who had lost his college love, pride, and spiritual direction. Vincent did not return for his second year.

Neema felt terrible about using Vincent but had to admit that she got some degree of satisfaction from the ruse more than a few times. "What goes around comes around. What Edith can do; I can do better. She took Nigel from me, and all I ended up with was a broken heart. I took Vincent from his fiancée, and now she has a broken heart. Life's a bitch!"

The end of Neema's first year in the Peace Corps was approaching and she hadn't figured out what to do during the summer break when the compound would be closed. Going back to Nashville was off the table. She needed a job and someplace to stay. She stared at the slogan pinned above her bed, "Making Up for Lost Time." Maybe her father or one of his former Ghanaian contacts knew someone who might help her. Neema came up with a better idea.

The next day, Neema made an appointment to see Dr. Charles Agbo, director of the Ghanaian Office for Foreign Public Affairs and the official government liaison for the Peace Corps. He had visited their compound on special occasions and had invited the group to Parliament House for meetings and social events. Neema hadn't been the only one who noticed when he openly flirted with her.

Charles Agbo was fifteen years Neema's senior and a sucker for a pretty woman. His father, Chief Nana Baffour Agbo, was head of a wealthy Ashanti royal family and proudly presided over important events and rituals like the Akwasidea Festival. She attended one of these festivals and saw Ago sitting on the Golden Stool and decked out in his elaborate Kente cloths. He wore gold rings on each finger, and gold bracelets circled his arms from his wrists to his elbows.

The Agbo's wealth had skyrocketed after his forefathers leased their gold mines to their former British colonizers. Those assets had afforded Charles Agbo a European education, a prestigious government job, and a portfolio of rental houses, hotels, and complicated business dealings in Africa, the Caribbean, South America, and Europe. However, Dr. Agbo was more than a wealthy portfolio. He was fine – handsome, smartly dressed, sexy, and confident. Neema had initially thought that Dr. Agbo might be a potential suitor, but after snooping around she discovered that he was married with two children and a pregnant wife, and she had lost interest. Still, Dr. Agbo might be able to help her find lodging and a job.

Dr. Agbo was delighted to see Neema. She wasn't sure if his enthusiasm was because she needed his help after having ignored his earlier advances, or if he was bored with his current roster of mistresses and looking for a new challenge. Whatever the reason, he quickly found Neema a position in the Department of Public Relations and a free room at one of his family's hotels. The job entailed typing, filing, and arranging events for visiting dignitaries. The living arrangement was minimal, but she knew the deal and waited for the late-night knock on her door. It took Charles ten days, and it wasn't a knock on the door. One evening when she came in from work there was a large envelope waiting for her at the hotel's front desk.

Her first thought was that Mr. Siriboe, her boss, had sent work for her to do at home. Shaking her head in disgust, she tore open the envelope. As she leafed through the contents, her anger dissipated. Enclosed was an official letter assigning her to an event in London, an airline ticket, the required diplomatic papers, and a hotel reservation. Well, I'll be damned! Neema smiled. Charles is slick. This is going to be one fun ride!

* * * * *

London was the first of the four trips she took that summer. She also visited Cape Town, Amsterdam, and Cairo. The rendezvous were perfectly executed, no doubt from practice. When Charles had business in a city, Mr. Siriboe would make Neema's travel arrangements. She and Charles never shared the same flight itinerary, never stayed in the same hotel, and never dined or appeared together in public. Since she had no real job responsibilities on these trips, Neema spent her time visiting sites like the Van Gogh Museum, Dutch windmills and canals, Table Mountain, The Hague, and the Great Pyramid of Giza. In London, she explored the British Museum, home to the world's largest collection of African artifacts. For centuries European colonizers systematically stole valuable cultural objects from countries throughout Africa and either sold them or shamelessly displayed them in their museums. She was particularly appalled by the more than six thousand items the British Museum had from the Ashante tribe, and she was eager to share her discovery with Charles.

"You should have seen how much art the British stole from Africa," she said, "and so many of the sacred artifacts were from the Ashante – golden swords, finger rings, masks . . . You wouldn't believe all the things they have. I am so angry! There must be some way that your government can get these items back to Ghana, right?"

"Why do you ask so many questions, Neema?" His voice softened. "First things first. Look what I bought you."

He opened a box and placed a red lace bra and matching crotch-less panties on the bed.

The playbook never varied regardless of what part of the world they were in. Charles would arrive after 11:00 p.m., order room service, eat, get undressed, hastily make love, and leave. It wasn't exactly "slam, bam, thank you ma'am," but it wasn't far from it.

At first Neema shrugged off what she considered to be mild irritations with Charles. After all, she reasoned, she was getting more than she was giving. But by the time she returned to Accra from her last "assignment," she wasn't so sure. She felt dirty and ashamed.

The failure of her "Making Up for Lost Time" plan hit her in the head like a two-by-four one evening in early August. Summer break was almost over and it would soon be time to return to the Peace Corps compound. Neema had completed her last summer assignment, a public relations reception for the visiting Prime Minister from Trinidad and Tobago and was exiting the ballroom to return to her hotel room. She noticed Charles holding court with someone in the corner whose face she could not see. She tried to sneak out, but he saw her.

"Miss Washington, come here. Glad I caught you. I have someone I want to introduce you to."

The man turned around and Neema went numb. Not only could she not respond, she could barely breathe.

"Miss Washington, please meet our unexpected guest, Minister Nigel Waite III of Jamaica. He was just telling me that he graduated from Howard University. Maybe you know him?"

At the exact moment that Nigel gave a hesitant smile and answered yes, Neema frowned and said no. Neither could look each other in the eye. Neema fidgeted with the silver bangles on her wrist, trying not to look as flustered as she felt.

Charles was too busy pontificating to notice.

"Nigel here is Jamaica's Minister of Government and Community Development," he said, "and his lovely wife is the Minister of Finance. *The Gleaner* newspaper said that their wedding was the biggest social event since Queen Elizabeth's visit in 1953! Pity I couldn't clear my calendar to attend."

Nigel had blocked out Agbo's chatter and was staring at Neema in disbelief.

"Neema, what a surprise. What are you doing here? You should stop by the embassy so that we can catch up. Please, please Neema. I need to talk to you."

"I don't think so," Neema said angrily, and she walked out of the ballroom.

Agbo, no stranger to awkward encounters between lovers, quickly sized up the situation. A domineering and jealous man, he liked to keep his women in check.

"Well, Nigel, you can forget about that one. I understand she's about to get married to one of her colleagues in the Peace Corps. Very promising young man. They seem much in love."

* * * * *

As she walked the streets of Accra, Neema ignored the drenching rain and roaring winds of the summer storm. She was already drowning in her own tears. The fact that she had been trying to avoid for years had caught up with her – she was still in love with Nigel. It was also true that she never wanted to see him again.

Neema reviewed the three reasons she had joined the Peace Corps – to find Aunt Eni, forget Nigel, and figure out how to live the rest of her life. She had failed miserably with the first two goals. Now she was determined to forge ahead on the third.

Neema threw herself into her Peace Corps work. She knew the culture, and her parents, Aunt Eni, and the Turner church family had shown her how to connect with people. In addition to her Peace Corps assignment, she volunteered with the local women in their efforts to eradicate malaria, immunize children, and educate girls. Her dedication, energy, intelligence, eloquence, and ability to connect with uneducated citizens, intellectuals, and political leaders caught the attention of high-ranking Peace Corps officials in the States as well as in other African countries. Neema was surprised by the attention. While obsessive twelve-hour days were interpreted as fidelity to the values and mission of the Peace Corps, they were just a cover. Neema was cramming her days in order to leave no time to think about Nigel and his wife.

In 1972, Neema's last year in the Peace Corps, she was encouraged to apply to the renowned School of International Studies at American University in Washington, DC. She was accepted and awarded the prestigious Sargent Shriver Peace Corps Graduate Fellowship.

*****

Neema had conflicting feelings about returning to Washington, DC. On the one hand, she was looking forward to reconnecting with Rose, one of her best friends from college. Still unmarried, Rose had completed her law degree at Harvard and landed a competitive job at DC's highly respected Public Defender Service. Neema knew their friendship would pick up where it had left off without missing a beat. She would miss Faye, though, who was married, living in California, and expecting her first child. On the other hand, DC was full of reminders of Nigel and the good times they had there together. One place she didn't want to see was Howard University.

There were only ten full-time students in Neema's graduate program at American University, and she was the lone Black student. This was a new experience for her. Her first three years of school were in Accra where all her classmates were Ghanaian. She was in all-Black segregated schools in Nashville for grades four through twelve, and then she went to Howard, where she had some white professors but never any white students in her classes. It would take a moment to get used to the idea of having white classmates, but Neema was excited to be in a challenging intellectual environment and knew that she'd quickly adjust.

One of the first classes she took was Cultural Anthropology. The professor opened his lecture with a discussion on cultural ethnocentrism, the tendency of Americans to view their culture as superior to others. He explained that most Americans had little knowledge of or experience with Asian and African countries, and that their inexperience and myopic perspective led them to believe that indigenous cultures were inferior.

"Unfortunately," he said, "once indigenous people are exposed to Western culture, particularly Africans, these people also start to believe that their way of life is inferior."

Neema carefully considered her response before she raised her hand. She didn't want to get off on the wrong foot with the professor the first week of the first semester.

"Dr. Reese, do you think that how Africans view themselves might depend more on their tribal affiliations?"

She was thinking about how Charles Agbo, an Ashante, was dismissive of other tribes in Ghana like the Fante and of African Americans because they were descendants of slaves.

"Miss Washington, as you read more and gain exposure to the literature, you will discover the subtle distinctions and more nuanced differences between cultures."

During class breaks, Neema's fellow students bombarded her with questions in their clumsy attempts to figure out the source of her intelligence and confidence. Her light skin and hair texture only added to their confusion; they couldn't decide if she was Hispanic or Middle Eastern. When she told them that she was born in Ghana, grew up in Nashville, and graduated from Howard University, they had even more questions: Where are your parents from? Did they send you to private schools up North? Neema decided to be cordial but knew she had to find the other Black students at American University. Fortunately, it didn't take long. She quickly hit it off with another doctoral student named Vanessa who had graduated from Spelman College. They had a lot of fun laughing about their many similar experiences attending an historically Black college.

Neema sailed through her two-year doctoral program, which included two internships at the US State Department, one in Policy Studies and the other in African Affairs. When she graduated in 1974, she had three job offers. She accepted the one from the State Department's Office of West African Affairs.

One day at work, Neema received an embassy communiqué from Jamaica. Inside the official envelope was a nondescript birthday card from the one person she had expected to never hear from again – Nigel.

Hope all is well, he wrote. *I found you through our international embassy documents. Sorry you ran away when I saw you in Accra. Would like to catch up. Nigel.*

The missing complimentary close, like "your friend," "sincerely," "regards," "take care," was a clue to Neema that he was uncertain about what he should say.

After the initial shock of reading Nigel's card, memories of their relationship at Howard University sent Neema on a roller coaster ride of emotions. She couldn't deny that a part of her was as excited as a teenager getting a Valentine's Day card from her first crush, but she knew that it would be a mistake to respond.

Neema liked her work and steadily moved up in the State Department, eventually becoming the assistant director of the Education Division. As one of a handful of Black women administrators, Neema often found herself marginalized, ignored, and insulted. Even though she had been hired because of her impressive academic records at Howard and American universities and had both lived in and been an outstanding Peace Corps volunteer in Ghana, her white supervisors expected her to be grateful for her job and compliant. Her colleagues and supervisors thought she was an "affirmative action hire" and therefore unqualified. She refrained from rolling her eyes or cursing people out when they made offensive comments, like "You're so well-spoken," and "What do Black people think about this?" and "Why do you always bring up race? I don't see color." And then there was the paternalistic, condescending comment that really made her blood boil: "Your people must be so proud of you!"

There was one other Black woman, a clerk, in Neema's division. Ethel was ten years older than Neema, five inches shorter, twenty pounds heavier, several shades darker, and always wore a red wig. Incredibly, their white co-workers were always getting the two women confused.

Neema particularly loathed meeting with her all-white, mostly male cohort group of division heads. Her ideas were seldom validated by the group and frequently attributed to some other colleague. Once when the group was brainstorming about the high rate of dropouts in African rural schools, particularly among pre-adolescents, Neema suggested that the conventional model of requiring students to sit in classrooms where teachers lecture and there is little or no student interaction was obsolete, ineffective, and contrary to African cultural traditions that encourage participation.

"Perhaps we should explore smaller, more intimate, community-identified spaces," she suggested, "like churches, sports fields, parks, rural and city communal areas."

For the next fifteen minutes, the group discussed the pros and cons of several other intervention strategies. Finally, one of her male colleagues got everyone's attention.

"You know what? We need to think outside of the box. We're stuck in a way of thinking that's like trying to fit a round peg into a square hole. Why don't we re-imagine what a classroom could look like?"

The man sitting across the table from him beamed. "Bob, you know I think you're on to something."

Neema sat stone-faced and dismayed. *Give me a break!* She didn't know if this type of behavior was racist or sexist or intentional or subconscious. It didn't matter. It was infuriating.

Less than a year after being promoted to assistant director, Neema was asked by her supervisor, Dr. Bianco, to write up her thoughts on a proposal focused on increasing literacy in village schools. Neema saw this as an opportunity to help her division understand the need for a new way of thinking about the problem. In her report, she pointed out how the agency's "build a school and they will come" approach discounted culturally specific barriers that limited educational opportunities, specifically for women and girls. Very little progress could be made, she predicted, if the agency continued to ignore difficult and uncomfortable conversations about rape, early pregnancies, arranged marriages, child labor, female genital mutilation, and cultural traditions like having sex with virgins to cure diseases. Neema knew that Aunt Eni had been subjected to this type of abuse as had several of the girls and women who had attended her mother's reading clinic in Accra. In her paper, Neema also proposed a bottom-up rather than top-down planning process that would involve tribal leaders like juju men, who were respected healers and spiritual advisors, and local government officials. She had often tagged along with her father when he visited various neighborhoods around Accra and saw how connecting with and gaining the trust of the grassroots facilitated his church work.

The pushback from Dr. Bianco was immediate.

"Miss Washington, I'm afraid you have a lot to learn about how we operate in my division. We are a team that supports each other. I thought you understood that. I took a chance when I asked you to respond to the proposal because you are the first upper-level minority in this division, and I was giving you a chance to present yourself to a wider audience. I'm very disappointed that instead you used this opportunity to undermine my initiatives. We'll continue this discussion later."

While Neema awaited her fate, her written report made its rounds through unofficial backchannels and caused quite a stir among staff, some of whom supported her views as well as those who didn't. By the time Dr. Bianco summoned her back to his office, Neema had become weary of negotiating subtle and not-so-subtle racist attacks, and so she had her letter of resignation in hand. She had no idea what she would do to support herself until she found another job but had decided to spare herself the agony of a prolonged appeal process if she was terminated. The meeting, however, had an unexpected outcome. Dr. Bianco explained that rather than initiating a long and complicated dismissal, he had agreed to transfer Neema to another office where the director, who had read her report, specifically requested her to join his team. In her new position, Neema would develop training manuals and professional development programs for agency staff and embassy personnel in six West African countries. Neema gladly accepted.

This was Neema's dream job, and for the next twenty years she happily traveled to Africa many times and accepted short-term, temporary assignments at any African consulate that wanted to advance her culturally responsive approach to literacy and schooling. She worked hard and avoided attachments and complicated relationships that might slow her down when opportunities crossed her path. Her "no drama" program included no mortgage, no pets, no needy friends, and no serious love affairs.

Neema was no anti-social misanthrope, though. She had many like-minded friends in DC with whom she shared similar interests, in particular Rose; Vanessa, her friend from American University; Eloise, who worked in another division at the State Department; and Vickie, who owned two Afrocentric bookstores. The women made it a point to gather monthly at The Mojo, an intimate, smoky club in DC's Adams Morgan neighborhood, to hear local and nationally recognized jazz musicians. The hostess stand barely cleared the opened front door. The massive bar with stools swallowed the entire upper level. Five narrow steps led down to the stage level, crammed with small circular tables and wood chairs with narrow seats that refused to comfortably accommodate the ample behinds of many of the Black women patrons. Finding their reserved seats required some skill. The women would have to walk sideways, hugging their purses to their chests, lest they hit someone in the head, knock over a drink or, Lord forbid, put their butts in somebody's face. Vickie, who wore a size sixteen dress at her thinnest, never quite mastered the last task.

The stage was just a slightly raised platform in front of a curtain that unsuccessfully tried to hide a tangle of electrical cords, folding chairs, music stands, mics, and amplifiers. Nevertheless, the instrumentalists and singers used this spartan space to produce soul-stirring music that invigorated and delighted the crowd. The club was a popular spot for making love connections, meeting new people, discussing work, or catching up with friends, but The Mojo was first and foremost about some unforgettable music.

Neema and Rose were also part of another social group that met at the Sankofa Theater Company in DC's Petworth neighborhood. The theater crew consisted of several community agency heads, college professors, and local and federal government workers who loved to intellectualize the Black Power Movement. They enjoyed attending plays and readings by noted writers of the Black Arts Movement like Ntozake Shange and Amiri Baraka as well as newcomers like Pearl Cleage. Afterward, they would hang out at one of the nearby restaurants to drink, eat, laugh, and argue about DC politics, Malcolm X, the Nation of Islam, and the Black Panthers. Neema especially enjoyed these outings because they gave her an excuse to wear some of the beautiful clothes and accessories that she had purchased in Africa or that she bought at various Black arts festivals around the country. Neema's collection included embossed leather purses by Marvin Sin, ivory jewelry by Densua, and uniquely styled indigo clothes by Damali. Neema tamed her natural hair with bobby pins and headbands at work, but on nights out with either of her crews she liberated her beautiful hair into a spectacular Afro.

Neema had no trouble attracting men to satisfy her sexual desires, but she avoided those who wanted exclusive, long-term relationships. She gravitated to single men who wanted to stay that way. She did, however, have a "stand by" lover, Dr. Jamal Alexander. They had met in 1987 at the annual meeting of the African Studies Association in New York where they shared the stage as symposium panelists. When Neema first saw him walk in the auditorium door, she did a double take. The brother had the same confident Black man's swagger that Nigel did! As he came closer, she noticed his smooth dark skin, beautiful smile, and neatly shaved mustache. His Afro perfectly framed his face.

"Are you saving this seat?" he asked. Before she could answer, he sat down next to her.

"I'm Jamal Alexander, chair of African and African American Studies at the University of

Maryland. Perhaps you know my predecessor, Amani Butler?"

They chatted about their mutual acquaintance until the session started. Each of their papers was well-received by the audience and their fellow panelists. During the question-and-answer session, Neema and Jamal got into a polite disagreement about some abstruse point related to the influence of W.E.B. Du Bois and C.L.R James in the Pan-African movement. The debate ended when the panel moderator cut them off. After the session, Jamal suggested they continue the discussion over a glass of wine in the hotel lobby.

By the time the week-long conference ended, Neema had slept with Jamal three times. She was not disappointed. After their first sexual encounter, Jamal had directed Neema's attention to his wedding ring.

"Of course, I saw it," she said. "I'm not blind."

Jamal started a familiar tale about his unhappy marriage and the two young children he loved. She stopped him mid-sentence.

"Spare me, Jamal. I don't want to hear about your marriage, your wife, or your kids. I enjoy your company. You're smart, engaging, well-read, funny, and discreet. So let's leave it at that. It works for me." She could tell he was a bit dubious. "Don't worry," she assured him, "I'm not going to call you or show up at your front door. I'm just glad we shared time together. Perhaps I'll see you at next year's conference."

Neema couldn't wait to call Rose and tell her about Jamal.

"Okay, Neema, this man is married. Where is this going?"

"That's the point, Rose. It's going nowhere. The man checks off all the boxes. He's fine, a great lover, smart, considerate, and—"

"And what?" Rose asked. "The man's married!"

"Don't worry, Rose. This was practically a one-night stand. By the way, aren't women allowed to have flings? I'll never hear from him again."

So Neema was surprised when Jamal called her at work two weeks later. That call led to a long-term relationship with a man she enjoyed but didn't love. When he could get away, he'd come over and they'd order food, drink wine, have sex, watch a movie, and sometimes argue about books and articles they'd read. Like clockwork, he always left for home at 8:00 p.m. Neema was not unhappy with the arrangement.

There was just one glitch. Since 1972, Nigel had continued to send a birthday card every year. Each had a similar prosaic Hallmark message and no closing, just his signature. She wasn't sure how she felt about the cards, but she kept them in their envelopes in a box in her office. She never re-read them, threw them away, or contacted Nigel.

CHAPTER FIVE

NASHVILLE, TENNESSEE LITTLE ROCK, ARKANSAS

Christmas season was the one time that Neema really looked forward to going home to Nashville. This was when, for the Washington family, the house rule was "Let There Be Peace on Earth." Neema would always arrive on December 20th and stay until January 2nd.

The tree decoration ritual hadn't changed since Neema was a child. The family would head out the night she arrived and ride around to different tree lots searching for the perfect tree. When they agreed on one, Joseph would tie it securely on top of the car and, once home, place it in a stand in front of the picture window in the living room. While Lily arranged the tree skirt around the stand and poured cups of eggnog for everyone, Joseph would retrieve the boxes of decorations from the basement. Joseph was the official disc jockey, playing album after album of Christmas music. They sang along and laughed a lot, occasionally at Neema, who hadn't inherited her parents' vocal skills. Each ornament had a backstory that got repeated every year as it was being hung.

"This was my mother's favorite," Lily would say as she found a place on the tree for the silver reindeer.

"I remember when Aunt Eni made this one," Neema would say.

"Remember when we bought this beaded one in Kumasi?" Joseph would ask Lily.

"Of course, I do." Rummaging through the boxes, she'd pick out the one with the Fisk mascot on it. "And do you remember when you gave me this one?" They'd both smile fondly at the shared memory. Then Lily would hand Neema the ornament with Howard Bison written on it. It was plain compared to the others, but Neema liked seeing her college represented on the tree.

After hours of hanging ornaments and stringing lights, Lily would bring out the wrapping paper, ribbon, bows, and scotch tape. This was Joseph's clue to retreat to his office. "All right, ladies," he'd say as he gave a quick salute, "have a good time."

The night of Christmas Eve was spent preparing fruit salad, a tradition passed down for generations in Lily's family. It wasn't so much of a salad as it was a punch bowl full of fruit. It was served whenever any of the Washington's many holiday visitors stopped by. The salad required the tedious task of peeling and cutting up fresh oranges and grapefruits with diced canned pineapple chunks, peaches, fruit cocktail. Probably because of all the citric acid, the fruit never spoiled. The longer the salad sat in the refrigerator, the better it got.

They always took down the Christmas tree a few days before the end of the month. This was not an option. A lot of Black Southerners believed that it was bad luck to keep the tree up after New Year's Eve. Most Black people, including the Washingtons, didn't really believe this superstition, but they didn't want to take the chance that it just might be true. The other holiday superstition that just about everyone observed was eating black-eyed peas and collard greens on New Year's Day. A generous serving of each guaranteed luck and prosperity in the coming year.

On New Year's Day in 1990, Neema and Lily were preparing the traditional meal when Lily asked Joseph to go to the grocery store to buy another can of black-eyed peas. After an hour, when Joseph hadn't returned, Lily began to get concerned.

"Where is your father, Neema? If he doesn't get back soon, the turkey will be cold. Not like him to stay gone to the store so long."

Neema offered to go find him. Just as she was reaching for her coat, the doorbell rang. It was a Nashville policeman. "I'm looking for Rev. Washington's wife."

"Sure, I'll go get her. By the way, I'm Neema, Rev. Washington's daughter. What's the problem?"

"I need to speak to your mother."

Neema went into the kitchen and told her mother about the policeman. The officer got right to the point. "My name is Officer Randall. Your husband had a medical emergency at the Piggly Wiggly and was taken by ambulance to the emergency room at Nashville General. Please go there right away."

"Oh my God!" Lily screamed.

As Neema drove to the hospital, Lily managed to speak one word, "Pray." No other word could be spoken.

"We're here to see Rev. Joseph Washington," Lily told the emergency room receptionist. "He arrived by ambulance about an hour ago. What's his room number?"

The receptionist flipped through a stack of papers. "Just a minute. I'll be right back. I have to find someone to help you."

"Miss, I don't need anyone to help me find a room in this hospital. What's the room number?" Neema demanded.

She returned with another woman who said, "Follow me, please." She opened the door to a small room. "Have a seat. Dr. Madison will be with you shortly."

Neema and Lily sat in silence, both lost in thoughts but trying not to think about the worst possibilities. The room was very odd. There was nothing in it but a wooden table with no drawers and two chairs that didn't match. There were no file cabinets, degrees on the wall, no medical equipment or supplies, and most disconcerting, no chair for the doctor to sit in.

Lily asked Neema, "What do they use this strange looking room for?"

The sudden opening of the door startled them. Dr. Madison quickly introduced himself and explained the situation with Joseph. He kept his hands in the pockets of his white coat while he talked.

"Mrs. Washington, and I assume this is your daughter?" Lily nodded. "I am sorry to inform you that Mr. Washington is gone."

"Gone?" Lily asked. She turned to Neema. "What's he saying? Gone? Gone where?"

Doctor Madison continued. "I'm sorry for your loss. Mr. Washington died of a massive heart attack inside the grocery store. The ambulance arrived within minutes, but their efforts to revive him were unsuccessful. I'm so sorry. Whenever you're ready, a nurse will escort you to identify his body. Take your time."

"No," Lily said, becoming indignant, "you're mistaken. My husband just went to buy some black-eyed peas. You have the wrong person."

"Mother," Neema said softly as she pulled her mother closer. "Daddy's left us." Tears streamed down her face like a waterfall.

"No!" Lily screamed. "Oh God, No! No!" Neema held Lily tightly.

When some time had passed, a nurse with a clipboard entered the room and requested routine information for the death certificate, the autopsy, and the release of the body to the funeral home. Without reading any of the forms, Lily signed them and then ordered, "Take me to see my husband now."

Joseph looked like he was taking a nap. He was still warm to the touch, and Lily and Neema kept stroking his cheeks and calling him softly.

"Joseph don't leave me. You're the love of my life."

"Daddy, I can't make it without you."

Neema sat in a chair at the foot of the bed and wept, alternating between resting her head on the edge of the mattress and staring at her father as though memorizing him.

Lily, too, was alternating between two actions. She would kiss her husband's cheek and whisper, "It's me, Joseph. Please stay with me." Then she would slowly walk to the other side of the bed, hold his hand, and pray, "Lord, have mercy." After an hour or so, Lily stooped beside Neema, who had her head on the mattress. "Your father's cold now. He's gone. Let's go home."

* * * * *

With the help of the church secretary, Lily and Neema managed to arrange Joseph's funeral. The funeral director tried to shame them into buying a package "suitable for a man of Rev. Washington's stature," showing them an assortment of high-priced coffins made from cherry wood, steel, and fiberglass with expensive linings and ornate metal handles. Neema got straight to the point.

"Mr. Johnson, we're buying a coffin to put in the ground, not a car."

Embarrassed and grieving, Lily started to cry and hurriedly went outside. Neema caught up with her mother and promised to be more patient. Indeed, Neema had to practice a lot of patience over the next couple of days because her normally well-organized, take-charge mother had ceased functioning. Lily had no opinion about the funeral program, the casket spray, the repast, or the grave marker.

Two weeks after the funeral, Neema reminded her mother that she would be leaving soon to go back to DC and suggested that they begin sorting her father's clothes to donate to a homeless shelter.

"Don't you dare touch Joseph's things!" Lily screamed.

"Okay, Mother, calm down. I just want to do as much as I can while I'm here. When I leave, would you like some of the Missionary Society ladies to take turns staying with you at night?"

"Absolutely not! I don't want those women piddling around in my house. Neema, you're rushing me. Just let me grieve in my own time, in my own way. Please."

* * * * *

Neema's focus on the funeral arrangements and her inconsolable mother had postponed her own grieving. During the long car ride to DC, she finally had the space to release the pain that was choking her. She remembered feeling a similar sense of loss and panic when she was ten years old. Not long after they had moved to Nashville, Neema and Lily heard about the annual fair that was held in Russell County, about seventy miles away. The fair was for whites only, but to appease complaints from the Negro community, one day each year was reserved for colored children. When Joseph arrived, Neema begged him to take her. Both of Neema's parents thought that the segregated activity was offensive, but Neema really wanted to go. Lily and Joseph agreed to take her this one time.

Neema was not disappointed. She had never seen anything like it. The 25-acre fairground had farm animals on display and a petting zoo with baby sheep, rabbits, and chicks. Women were exhibiting flowers and Mason jars of jellies, peaches, and string beans, competing for coveted first-prize ribbons. Neema got to ride on the bumper cars, slide down the giant sliding board, and ride on the Ferris wheel, merry-go-round, and twirling teacups. She tried to eat a candy apple, but the impenetrable red candy coating proved too tough for her small teeth. She had more luck with the cotton candy that melted in her mouth and left her face a sticky mess. The family had a wonderful time.

Just as they were getting ready to leave, Neema spotted the House of Mirrors.

"Oh, Mother, Daddy, that looks like fun! Can I go?"

"Sure, Honey, I'll go with you," Joseph said.

The House of Mirrors was an elaborate maze of convex and concave mirrors with confusing obstacles. Neema and Joseph laughed as they maneuvered through narrow aisles and saw how the mirrors distorted their reflections. Neema let go of Joseph's hand so she could wave her hands and dance in front of one mirror that elongated her head and one beside it that made her stomach look like an overinflated balloon on top of short legs. She turned to show her daddy, but when she looked around, she didn't see him anywhere. She immediately panicked.

"Daddy! Daddy, where are you? Daddy! Daddy!"

Neema tried to retrace her steps and when she didn't see Joseph, she turned and ran in the opposite direction, clumsily bumping into scary reflections of herself at each turn. She climbed a few steps that led to nowhere. She began to cry. Just then, Joseph appeared seemingly out of nowhere and scooped her up in his arms.

"Calm down, my Baby girl. I have you. You're safe. You never have to worry about being lost. I'll always be here for you."

Now Neema was without her anchor, consoler, and biggest cheerleader. Most importantly, her father's mere presence often de-escalated the tensions that frequently bubbled up between her and her mother. Neema was the first to back down because she noticed the pain in her father's eyes and his shallow breathing. She knew when he hastily retreated to his office and stared out of the bay window with his intertwined hands over his chest, he was praying for his family. He was the glue that held their small family together, and now, without warning, he was gone.

* * * * *

Lily stayed in her home after Joseph's death. Neema would fly or drive to Nashville at least once a month to help, but she would have preferred a different living arrangement for her mother. Neema knew Lily, at age 68, would refuse to live with her in DC or even in a nearby apartment. She was a small-town lady who would never drive, take a cab, or ride the Metro. The last time Lily was in DC, Neema took her on the Metro to see a play. Lily stared straight ahead to avoid eye contact with the homeless man walking up and down the aisle begging for money. She wrapped the straps of her shoulder bag around her forearm and hugged the purse close to her chest as if it was a crying infant. Lily grabbed Neema's arm when they exited the train because the handrails and hanging straps "were nasty." Of course, Neema reasoned, her mother would be lonely and miserable in DC. She did not make new friends easily. Neema never tested her conclusions about Lily's unwillingness to move. Neema never asked her because she knew her less-than-satisfying life would turn into a miserable one if her mother moved to DC.

A couple of years after her father's death, a solution to her mother's living arrangements appeared out of the blue, proving, as her mother often said, that the Lord works in mysterious ways.

Christine was Lily's first cousin, the daughter of her father's sister, Alfreda. Christine had begun calling Neema to vent about her situation. Having never married or had children, she was feeling lonely and increasingly isolated in Detroit. Her friends were either sick, had left Detroit to live near relatives, or dead. Christine wanted to move to Little Rock to build a house on part of the Robinson estate that she had inherited jointly with Lily from Grandfather Alfred. She asked Neema if she thought Lily would agree to partition the property so she could build.

Neema had a better idea. She convinced the two elderly cousins to pool their resources and build a shared home on the property. It wasn't an easy sell. First, Lily and Christine didn't really know each other. They had grown up in different cities, and they had lived very different lives. Second, neither of them really knew Little Rock. They each had a few vague memories but no real ties. Lily had left Little Rock at age seventeen to go to Fisk and, because of her strained relationship with her parents, rarely returned. Christine's connection was even more distant. Her mother, Alfreda, had left Arkansas in the 1950s during the latter part of the Great Black Migration to the North. After she settled in Detroit, she only took her family to Little Rock to visit once a year in the summer and every other Christmas. And third, Lily was still protective of her independence. It took some time before she, like Christine, began to feel the isolation of living alone.

Incredibly, Neema convinced the cousins that the move was in their best interests, and within two years they had settled into their new home. The custom ranch-style house had separate bedroom suites on each end, a guest room, kitchen, dining room, family room, and a car port that accommodated both of their cars. The huge screened-in porch with a ceiling fan offered tranquil views of tall pines, oaks, junipers, and a charming assortment of birds, deer, and rabbits. The cousins were in good health, made new friends, and were both active in the church that their grandparents had attended. Lily joined the choir and played the piano when the regular pianist was late or couldn't attend the service. Christine was a member of the Senior Usher Board. Neema was happy her plan had worked even though she had occasional pangs of guilt knowing that it had also relieved her of the burden of taking care of her mother.

Lily and Christine became active in The Mademoiselles, a social club, and both looked forward to its monthly meetings. The club members met in each other's homes, and the routine was always the same. The meeting would begin with Mabel, known as the prayer warrior, blessing the food, delivering a mini sermon about hungry people in faraway lands, and ending with a request for God to bless all the talented cooks in the room. Next, Dorothy, the president, would give a five-minute report on the latest plans for the group's only event, the annual Christmas party. Invariably, before Dorothy could finish, Maggie, who always seemed to be full of self-righteous indignation, would interrupt.

"Excuse me, excuse me," Maggie had said at the last meeting, waving her hand as though she was in school, "but we can't have that mess we had at last year's party. Ya'll saw Brother Matthews passing 'round a bottle of liquor he snuck in and getting close up in women's faces. We are Christian women, and this cannot happen this year!"

There was no resolution on what to do about Brother Matthews, but the club members enjoyed complaining and laughing about their "heathen" church member.

After they collected dues, the real meeting agenda began – laughing and gossiping. The most anticipated bit of news was always from Betty, whose husband owned the Black funeral home. As if on cue, Mae, Betty's sidekick, would ask, "So, what's going on down at the funeral parlor?"

"Girl," Betty said, "I'm glad you asked. You wouldn't believe how busy we been!"

She began by talking about who purchased the cheapest casket, who had the best-looking flowers, and whose relatives did or did not show up from out of town. Then she got to the real gossip.

"We had eight funerals at four different churches last month. I barely had time to breathe! But the one that really got to me was Chester Evans' funeral. You won't believe what I'm getting ready to tell ya'll."

The room fell silent and the women leaned forward. Betty continued.

"We were in the funeral home's reception room for the private family viewing, and things were moving along nicely. If I do say so myself, we did a good job on him. Chester looked just like himself. Anyway, when it was time for the visitors to join the family, guess who prances in with a skirt so tight you could see the crack in her butt?"

The women gave a collective gasp and held their breath.

"You ain't got to tell me," Mae said. "It had to be that hussy Brenda who lives on Conway Road near the Esso service station. Am I right?"

"Girl, you hit the nail on the head. Everybody knew she and Chester had a thang going on, but why would she show up like that?" Betty wondered. "Well, you know how Chester's wife Mattie is. She ended that mess before it got started. Jumped out of her chair in front of the casket and told that floozy to get the hell out of the funeral home. Then she told Brenda somebody would be planning her funeral if she showed up at Chester's service."

Mae gave her usual refrain, "Oh no-o-o- she didn't?" Betty responded as always, "Oh yes she did!"

The club members hooted and laughed as they imagined the scene. This went on until the club president said it was time to eat.

The Mademoiselles enjoyed breaking bread with their fellow club members and looked forward to this part of the meetings. It was a potluck meal and might include pimento cheese or tuna sandwiches cut in quarters and lime frappe punch with pineapple rings and maraschino cherries. But the stars of the meal were the cakes and pies, all homemade and delicious.

The biggest surprise about the cousins' move to Little Rock happened when Christine started keeping company with a widower she met at church. Her "male friend" would visit her on Sunday evenings to watch movies and eat freshly popped popcorn. Christine had never been happier.

Neema felt free now to live her life as she pleased, with a two-week visit during Christmas and New Year's, a week during the summer, and phone calls each Sunday afternoon. Neema patted herself on the back, "I can finally start living my life."

* * * * *

One day in 1994, two years after Lily moved to Little Rock and four years after Joseph's death, Neema was beginning an important meeting with her staff when she heard the conference room door squeak. She braced herself and breathed deeply. I don't believe that hussy just slipped into this conference room. Neema tried to maintain her professional mask, one of many she had perfected during her tortured life of forty-five years. Just twenty minutes ago, she asked Laura, her secretary, not to interrupt her staff meeting. Neema was pissed. What the hell could she possibly want now?

Laura's often-mocked grand entrances featured an overweight, big-boned, former DC block girl pretending to be invisible and obsequious. She squeezed through the cracked door that was much too narrow for her wide body stuffed in a dress that challenged the distinction between the office and the nightclub. The thirty-year-old divorcee claimed to be a sanctified church lady, but Neema had her doubts. Predictably, Laura peered over her cat-eye, leopard-print readers, pursed her lips tightly and scanned the room for her boss. Once Laura spotted Neema, she cast her eyes to the floor and slowly tip-toed toward her boss in spiked-heel, narrow-toed shoes that were clearly at odds with her size ten feet. With hips swaying rhythmically and suggestively, Laura placed the folded pink telephone message note on Neema's desk and tapped on it as if the twenty people in the conference room hadn't noticed her when she sashayed in. The men stared in anticipation for the rearview finale. Laura never disappointed.

Neema could have transferred Laura to another State Department office, but she knew exactly why she didn't. Laura reminded Neema of "Switching Miss Liz," making her late entry into her childhood home church in Nashville. Neema's mother stayed annoyed with Miss Liz, and Neema stayed annoyed with her mother. Neema admitted that her thinly veiled Freudian justification made no sense. But neither did her messed up life.

When the meeting ended, Neema stood up and the pink telephone message floated to the floor. Damn, she thought, I was so distracted by Laura's sideshow I forgot to read the note. The message was from Christine: *Call me right away. You need to come home to Little Rock immediately.*

It was still dark and chilly that fall morning when Neema pulled out of her condo parking space and headed south for a fifteen-hour drive to Little Rock. The farther she drove from DC, the more anxious she got. Neema couldn't believe how bad timing and bad luck followed her like some crazed stalkers who wouldn't give up. What was weighing most heavily on Neema was her job. She had recently applied for a promotion to West African Affairs in Accra, her dream job. This was a terrible time to be taking leave, but when she had explained to her supervisor that she had a family emergency, her boss had encouraged her to take the time. Maybe, she thought, she wasn't getting the promotion and they were just stalling telling her. It took Neema at least an hour of deep breathing and visualizing the beaches in Accra to calm down and refocus her attention on her mother and cousin's situation.

Neema was beginning to feel better as she sped down Interstate 81. She figured it would take less than a week to settle things down between Lily and Christine. She would hire some church sister to come in and help with the cooking, do the cleaning, and most importantly, referee the interactions between two difficult 70-year-olds. But Neema couldn't understand why Cousin Christine was sometimes teary and angry on the phone. Christine must be losing it, Neema concluded. Her mother sounded OK last week. Nothing seemed different. Lily's nonstop phone chatter hadn't changed over the previous five years. The topics never varied nor the adjectives used to describe them – the odd weather, the sorry preacher, stuffed up sinuses, crazy white people, the outrageous price of gas, tasteless grocery store tomatoes, or speeding cars on busy highways. Neema's frequent interjection, "What else is going on, Mother?" fell on deaf ears. Lily stuck to her script. The call always ended with the same question, "Neema, when are you coming to see me?"

Slowly at first, but with increasing alarm, things began to fall apart. Lily complained about Christine's cooking and housekeeping. Then, one day, an exasperated Christine awakened Neema from her usual Sunday afternoon nap.

"Neema, you won't believe what your mother asked me and my male friend last night. She asked if we were having sex! I thought I would faint. She blurts out anything that pops into her head. But that's not the worst of it. This morning she told the preacher's wife, in front of some ushers, that her new suit was not becoming. She actually asked the lady if she was gaining weight."

Neema always patronized or ignored their quarrels. Now she was headed to Little Rock to handle a deteriorating situation with only a vague notion of what she might find or how to fix it. No matter how hard she tried to focus on other things, the long and lonely highway crashed head-on into memory lane about her life of few joys and too many regrets. She felt claustrophobic. Was she getting bigger, or was the car shrinking?

She breathed deeply and then did something that surprised her. She prayed. Lord, help me take care of my mother. Give me strength and patience. Please Lord, give me wisdom and insight into my mother's life so I can figure out how to help her and be a better daughter.

* * * * *

Neema arrived at the Little Rock house early on Sunday evening. She always arrived after the 11:00 a.m. church service to avoid her mother's nagging about going to the service. Neema's late arrival also solved the Sunday brunch "all you can eat" problem. Lily and Christine would insist on taking Neema to some tacky restaurant buffet of inedible fried meat, fake cheese dishes, canned vegetables, and desserts that would send a diabetic into shock.

When Neema pulled into the cousins' front yard, she did not get the expected welcome home greeting. Usually, her mother would run out of the house as soon as she drove up, but this time the place seemed eerily quiet. Her mother's car was not in the carport. Neema rang the doorbell, and a hysterical Christine opened the door.

"Lily didn't show up for church today! We ate breakfast, and she left for Sunday School. I came later for the 11 o'clock service and didn't see her. It's 5 o'clock now, and no one has seen her. Neema, something is wrong. Lily would never miss Sunday School, Communion Sunday service, and the choir! I called the police."

Christine's words seemed to float from her lips in slow motion. Neema heard what Christine said but couldn't comprehend the meaning. She was stuck in place, like a deer caught in headlights.

"Neema, Neema," Christine shouted, "I don't know where Lily is!"

Neema tried to think of a plausible explanation for her mother's disappearance but couldn't. So, they wept together.

They both blamed themselves. Christine told Neema that she had noticed Lily's rapid decline six months ago. Lily asked the same questions and made the same observations. When Christine reminded Lily that she was repeating herself, she would become irritated. When Christine reminded her to eat her morning cereal, Lily claimed she already had. She was slowly losing weight. Christine dismissed Lily's decline and concluded she had "senioritis," like all other old folks.

Christine said Lily must have been aware of her condition because she became more introverted. When she went to church, Lily never called her familiar friends by their names. One weekday she dressed for church. Sometimes she appeared from her suite wearing the same clothes she had on the day before. Christine had tried to warn Neema with subtle phone calls that would not alarm her.

Your mother is out of sorts these days.

We miss you. When are you coming home?

Lily has just fired the yardman for no good reason.

I think Lily's blood pressure medicine has her upset all the time.

Lily's irritation slowly evolved into anger. She accused Christine of stealing her purse when she misplaced it. So, she walked around the house carrying her purse and hiding rolled-up bills in her bra. She cursed Christine and told her that her male friend was trying to get in her bed at night.

Christine begged Neema's forgiveness. "Neema, I am so sorry. I didn't know how to tell you these terrible things. I didn't know what to call her sickness." Neema assured Christine that she shouldn't blame herself.

On the other hand, Neema felt it was her fault. She literally and figuratively had run away from her mother. She focused on the only thing that made her feel good – her career.

Neema could not convince Christine to help her search for Lily. Christine wanted to obey the police's suggestion that she stay at home and wait until his office contacted her. Neema, not accustomed to waiting or following orders, was losing patience. "You stay here, Christine. I'm going to find my mother."

Neema sat in her car for fifteen minutes before concluding she had no idea where to start looking. As she exited her vehicle, a state trooper drove up in the yard. Lily was found thirty miles north of Little Rock, sitting in her car in a K-Mart parking lot. She was confused, hungry, and wet from urinating on herself. Otherwise, she appeared okay. The local police transported Lily by ambulance to St. Vincent's Hospital.

Lily was heavily sedated when Neema and Christine arrived. After a couple of hours, Neema convinced Christine to go home to rest, and she settled in for the night. Around 3:00 a.m., Lily stirred.

"Oh, Neema," she said brightly, "What are you doing in Nashville? Where am I? Go get your father and tell him to take us home."

Lily dozed off and on all night, and each time she woke up she asked Neema to get Joseph for her.

The following day, Lily seemed to be thinking a bit more clearly, and Neema was relieved. Lily was doing her usual chatter about the odd weather and gas prices and tasteless tomatoes when she brought up a new topic.

"Neema," she said, "you look just like your granddaddy."

Neema corrected her. "No, Mother, you must be confused. You always say I look like my grandmother, remember? How we both have the same thick, wavy hair and light skin?"

"No," insisted Lily. "Your grandmother wasn't light-skinned. It was your granddaddy. He was half-white."

"Okay, Mother," Neema said good-naturedly, not wanting to upset her, "if you say so."

Lily stayed in the hospital for three days of observation, tests, and consultation with her primary care physician, a young white man. He took Neema and Christine out into the hallway and confirmed what was obvious. Lily had Alzheimer's disease.

"But let's talk about the other major health issue that Lily is dealing with," the doctor said.

"Please refer to my mother as Mrs. Washington," Neema instructed. Christine looked embarrassed. "What other issue?"

"Oh, I assumed she had told her family. A year ago, Mrs. Washington was diagnosed with stage four pancreatic cancer."

Neema and Christine looked at each other in shock.

"At the time," the doctor continued, "chemotherapy and radiation were not feasible remedies. As I explained to your mother, the average survival rate for this type of cancer for a woman her age is between two and six months. She's beat the odds so far, but I think she only has a few months left. I am recommending that she be transferred to a hospice." Neema and Christine were inconsolable.

The next day, a solemn Neema rode with her mother in the ambulance to Caring Hearts, a hospice that marketed itself as a peaceful, home-like setting for the final transition. Neema hated euphemisms like transition, passing, expiring, crossing over, and going home for death, as if using different words eased the pain. There was nothing in Caring Hearts that reminded anyone of a home, with its drab grey décor, scuffed linoleum hallways, artificial plants, and smell of Lysol disinfectant. It was the epitome of institutionalized dying.

While Neema was getting Lily settled into her new room, Lily started whispering.

"Neema, where am I? Please, take me home. Who stole my purse? Get Joseph and tell him to find Miss Ruby. I need her to help me fix this."

Neema was confused. She'd never heard of Miss Ruby and didn't even know if she was a real person or not.

"Mother, who is Miss Ruby? Is she one of your church members? I can ask Christine to bring her if you'd like to see her."

"Oh, Neema, you know Miss Ruby, your grandmother. Ask Rev. Harper. He'll bring her."

Lily kept repeating and repeating and repeating that she wanted to see Miss Ruby. The nurse thought that Lily might be tired and suggested that Neema leave so her mother could get some rest.

Neema couldn't wrap her head around the fact that her mother's life was ending this way. For the first time in a long time, she wished that she had a sibling or a significant other to help her cope with all of this. She called Rose.

"Girl, I can barely hold it together," she said, her voice cracking.

The friends talked for hours. Even though Neema was finally able to get some sleep, she felt depressed and exhausted and couldn't get out of bed the next day, and so Christine went to stay with Lily.

Neema assumed that Ruby was one of her mother's friends and that Rev. Harper was either also a friend or maybe a pastor at one of the local churches. When Christine returned home from Caring Hearts, Neema asked her for their addresses and phone numbers. Christine had no idea who these people were, but she was pretty sure that they weren't from Little Rock.

Neema informed her job that she would be using four weeks of leave to attend to her mother. Throughout the first two weeks, Neema listened as her mother endlessly asked for her parents, for Joseph, and for Miss Ruby. She kept warning Neema not to go to Ghana, where women, she claimed, try to break up happy homes. And she was adamant about Neema finding her alleged grandmother, Miss Ruby. When Neema tried to get more information about Miss Ruby and Rev. Harper, Lily would close her eyes and refuse to talk.

Neema usually left the hospice around 9:00 p.m. when her mother fell asleep. This night, though, she had a strong urge to return to her mother's bedside, so she turned around in the parking garage and walked back inside. To Neema's surprise, when she entered her mother's room, Lily was awake and smiling.

"Neema, it's time for me to go home now," she said in a strong voice. "Joseph is waiting for me. He was a good father and husband, and I loved him dearly. Neema, he betrayed me once in Accra with some Howard University Jezebel from New York. It broke my heart, but I forgave him for all the pain he caused and let him come back into our family. In the end, we were at peace."

Neema was awash in feelings – shocked that her father had been unfaithful, disappointed that he hadn't always been the saintly man she thought him to be, sorry that her mother had been hurt so badly, and angry that she hadn't been more compassionate to her. If there was one emotion she knew only too well, it was the pain of being betrayed by the man you love.

"I love you so much, Neema. You are the best gift I ever received. You know what your name means in Swahili, don't you?"

"Yes, Mother – Grace."

"That's right, amazing Grace, and you are amazing! Now go find Miss Ruby." Lily mustered the energy to sing her favorite line from the hymn, "Grace has brought me safe thus far, and grace will lead me home."

Usually when Lily hummed or sang *Amazing Grace*, it meant that she was content. Neema prayed that she would live to sing it many more times.

"Mother," she said, "you want me to find Miss Ruby and Rev. Harper, but I don't know where to look. Where are they?"

Lily closed her eyes. "Pope City, your grandparents live in Pope City, Georgia."

Two hours later, Lily Robinson Washington died. It was Mother's Day.

* * * * *

Neema's return to work was difficult. Well-meaning colleagues overwhelmed her with condolences, some even burdening her with stories of their own personal grief. She was hoping that she would easily pick up her life when she came back to DC, but nothing felt the same. Her grief, anger, and guilt trapped her in a dark place and made it hard for her to breathe. She kept asking herself, what kind of daughter was I? Like every Black woman, she knew that daughters were expected to care for elderly parents. Sons got a pass. The unwritten rule was that caring and sacrificing were women's burdens to bear, especially if they were single and childless. Many Black families either couldn't afford or were opposed to putting their parents in nursing homes and instead expected daughters to move them into their homes. Neema understood these long-held mores but had always refused to let these gender-biased expectations confine or define her. But she acknowledged the apparent contradictions of her current circumstances. She was feeling very guilty.

Her mother's last few hours haunted her. Why, on her deathbed, would she tell me about Daddy's affair, a revelation that would stain Neema's memory of her father forever? And then there was the preposterous story about her grandparents being the Harpers in Pope City. Evidently, Miss Ruby was married to Rev. Harper. Why would her mother continue to insist that some people she'd never heard of were her grandparents? She tried to convince herself that both stories were the result of her mother's dementia. Still, the one about the Harpers led Neema to think of another troubling possibility. If Joseph's parents weren't her grandparents, then Joseph wasn't her father.

Rose was concerned about her friend. Neema refused to go out, and sometimes she wouldn't answer the phone or return calls. She knew that Neema needed time alone to grieve her mother's death, but as more and more time passed, she became more and more worried. Unable to restrain herself any longer, one day she knocked at Neema's door unannounced. When Neema finally opened the door, Rose was shocked. Neema was a wreck. She was forty-five years old, but her constant worrying had her looking ten years older. It was apparent that she hadn't showered or put on clean clothes or combed her hair in days, and Rose suspected she hadn't been eating much either. She immediately went to work cleaning Neema's condo, buying food, and persuading her friend to go out for a walk. At Rose's insistence, Neema began going to therapy.

CHAPTER SIX

POPE CITY, GEORGIA

With counseling, Neema was able to reconcile her father's infidelity. She knew that whatever had happened in Accra, her parents had worked it out and moved on. Their forty-seven-year marriage had been a good one. What she couldn't put to rest was her mother's allegation about her grandparents. The therapist suggested that she research her family tree. In the end, she worked on three family trees: the Robinsons of Little Rock, Arkansas; the Washingtons of Pope City, Georgia; and, just in case, the Harpers of Pope City, Georgia.

Neema was surprised by how much she enjoyed genealogy. She wanted to spend more time on this new project. Why can't I? Why do I have to be an exceptional, over-achieving African American woman, a credit to my race? She remembered Black parents told their children they had to be twice as smart and work twice as hard as white people to get ahead. The hell with that! she fumed. Last year the vice-president of the United States, Dan Quayle, couldn't spell potato. I can be average, like most white folks. I can do this job, finish by noon, and then work on my family's genealogy trees. Keeping the train on the tracks and on schedule became Neema's new standard.

Genealogy was challenging and fit her voracious intellect. If the information existed, she was determined to find it. Although she sometimes hit a brick wall or fell down the proverbial rabbit hole, each discovery was like hitting the jackpot. Neema was hooked, and the stakes were high. If there was a family secret, she was determined to find it.

In the evenings and on weekends, Neema poured over documents and microfilms in the National Archives in DC and the Mormon Family History Center in Maryland and attended local and national genealogy conferences. She was amazed by the extensive amount of information she was able to find for her three family trees without having to leave DC. She already knew a lot about the Washington and Robinson families, and when she needed more information, she would call one of her distant relatives. But she had to start from scratch with the Harpers.

Starting with the most recent US census and working backward with census data, newspaper obituaries, military records, divorce records, cemetery indexes, marriage licenses, birth and death certificates, city directories, high school and college yearbooks, and the AME church archives, Neema began to piece together the essential parts of the Harper family tree. When her parents had lived in Pope City, Rev. Robert Harper was the Presiding Elder of Joseph's father's church. He and his wife Ruby had four children: Lucille (born 1913), Eula (1914), Robert Jr. (1917), and Margaret (1935). She found Robert Jr.'s military records and his burial site in a veterans' cemetery in Georgia. Lucille only finished the sixth grade and married a preacher in her late teens. Neema assumed that Lucille was deceased, but she couldn't find a death certificate. Eula had married an Army soldier in 1940 and was buried in the same military cemetery as her husband and brother Robert. Margaret, the youngest child, was challenging to trace. She appeared in the 1940 census, but there were no records after that. Neema speculated that she might have died as a child, which wasn't unusual in those days. Neema was left with only one working hypothesis. If Robert and Ruby Harper were her grandparents, then her father had to be the Harpers' only son, Robert Harper, Jr.

Neema's head was spinning. So, my father had an affair with a woman in Accra, and my mother had an affair with a man in Pope City? Who *were* these people I called my parents? Evidently not the sainted folks I thought they were.

Lily used to like to testify about the difficulty she had had conceiving until God's amazing grace blessed her with a child. Now Neema wondered if she had, indeed, been a blessing from God. Maybe her father had been sterile, and her mother had sex with this Harper guy so that she could have a baby. Maybe her father had sanctioned the idea because he also wanted a baby or wanted to please his wife. Or maybe her mother deceived her father into thinking that Neema was his and that she got her skin complexion from his light-skinned mother-in-law.

Whatever the case, Neema was furious. The only chance she had of finding answers to her questions was to track down any surviving Harpers. She knew that Robert Jr. and Eula were deceased, but what about Lucille and Margaret? She needed to dig into the county records in Pope City, Georgia. It was August and Neema had been planning to go on vacation. Instead, she booked a flight to Atlanta, reserved a rental car for the 100-mile ride to Pope City, and made reservations for a week-long stay at the local Holiday Inn.

Neema had never been to Pope City but remembered sitting under the baobab tree listening to her father talk about growing up there. Many of his stories were about his father's church, Payne Chapel AME.

"Neema," he'd said proudly, "my hometown protected Black children from white people, and Payne Chapel was a sanctuary in more ways than one. My father preached that even though white people had power and were dangerous, they could never define us. And he told me something that I'll never forget. He said it more times than I can count, and I don't want you to forget it either. 'Son,' he'd say, 'ain't nothing wrong with you. White folks just crazy!'"

Rev. and Mrs. Washington, now deceased, left Pope City soon after Joseph and Lily had left for Africa. They returned to their hometown of

Birmingham, where Rev. Washington was promoted to Presiding Elder of the Northern Alabama AME district.

The drive to Pope City from Atlanta looked like all the other interstates in America – miles of monotonous roads surrounded by billboards and signs identifying exits for gas stations, weigh stations, convenience stores, tourist sites, and small towns most people had never heard of. When she finally pulled into the parking lot of Pope City's Holiday Inn, Neema sighed, resigned to the fact that this would be her live-work space for the next seven days. The two-story stucco building had a huge metal canopy over the lobby entrance and outside stairs on each side that led to the second floor. There were only five other cars in the parking lot. The young white man who checked Neema in couldn't refrain from asking her a series of rapid-fire questions.

"Where you from? Got folks 'round here? This your final destination?"

Neema was polite but curt. The clerk got the message and hurriedly completed checking her in.

Neema was prepared for the dingy room. She removed all the linen from the bed and replaced them with the one sheet and a pillowcase she had packed. Next, she generously sprayed every object in the room with her disinfectant spray. To give the room time to air out, she decided to find the church her father had told her about while sitting under the baobab tree, Payne Chapel.

Although she had a map, she was having difficulty finding the place. Figuring that every Black person in a small town like Pope City would know where all the Black churches were, she asked the next Black person she saw. Sure enough, she got excellent directions and was soon parked in front of the building. Much to Neema's surprise, a small group of older women were gathered on the steps of the church, and they turned to see who was about to get out of the car. It was a Monday afternoon and Neema hadn't expected to run into anyone, so she quickly weighed her options. If she got out and introduced herself, she'd probably have to answer more questions than she wanted to. If she asked them if any of the Harper family still lived in town, word would probably get back to the Harpers that some stranger was looking for them and might make them suspicious. Not sure what she should do, she eased out of the parking space and tried to look nonchalant as she drove away.

Neema got up early the next morning and headed for Crawford, the county seat for Pope City where all the vital records were housed. Crawford was just thirty miles away, but in less than ten minutes she had driven to what looked like the middle of nowhere. The highway had narrowed to two lanes and was hemmed in by acres of three-foot tall cotton bushes spaced about thirty inches apart with white blossoms that the uninformed and insensitive might describe as picturesque. Neema pulled over and got out of the car. The ninety-degree heat seared the asphalt road, producing an eerie haze. Neema could imagine emaciated slaves bending over to pick those blossoms and place them in the burlap bags they dragged between the rows. In her head she heard her parents singing one of their favorite songs, *Steal*

Away. This is too much, she thought, and she got back in the car and turned up the air-conditioner. The irony didn't escape her. I'll never understand how Black folks survived this, she thought.

The town square in Crawford was a well-kept grassy area in the middle of the town. Tall pine trees, crepe myrtles, and dogwoods lined the square's perimeter and provided shade for park benches. Across the street on one side stood the three-story neoclassical brick courthouse with a large domed clock tower that displayed the incorrect time. The portico had four granite columns, two on each side of the front entrance, and was home to a thirty-foot monument of a Confederate soldier kneeling near a canon with a musket in his hand. Neema frowned at the statue and at the huge Confederate flag that blew unapologetically on the flagpole in front.

The Office of Revenue and Tax Assessment was the first office Neema saw when she entered the building. She took a deep breath and prepared for another white person seeking confirmation to the annoying question, "You not from around here, are you?" She stood in front of the chest-high counter waiting for someone to appear until she noticed the well-worn call bell. She tapped it three times and a smiling young Black woman with braids came out of the back office. Not what Neema had expected.

"Hi, I'm Sarah Lewis, the assistant registrar. How can I help you?"

"Yes, thank you. My name is Neema Washington. I need to do a property search and tax record history for a house in Pope City. It was originally owned by Robert Harper."

"You're not from around here, are you?" Sarah asked.

Apparently, Neema thought, whites weren't the only nosey people down here.

Neema explained that her father had grown up in Pope City and that her grandfather, Rev. Washington, was once the pastor of Payne Chapel AME. She wanted to know more about a family that might be related to her, the Harpers. Sarah perked up. It turned out that she lived in Pope City and attended Payne Chapel. She told Neema that she knew the oldest living Harper, Miss Lucille, and her daughter, Constance.

"Constance brings Miss Lucille to church every now and then, but Miss Lucille's health is failing."

"What? You mean she's still in Pope City!" Neema's heart was racing. "I can't believe it." Neema wanted to jump up and shout but she didn't want Sarah to think she was crazy.

Now that the formalities were out of the way, Sarah was eager to help and soon was dragging out every dusty file folder and ledger she could find about Lucille Harper Johnson and the Harper house.

Between customers stopping in to pay tax bills, Neema and Sarah chatted like old friends. Neema explained that she only had a few days to do her research before she had to get back to her job in DC.

Looking around to be sure none of her white coworkers was spying on her, Sarah confided, "Girl, I know what you mean. White folks will work you to death and then take all the credit. Can get on your last nerve!" They laughed at their common cultural experiences.

By the time the office closed for the day, Neema had found out that in 1910, soon after he married Ruby, Rev. Harper had purchased the land that the family home still stood on. When they died, the estate was divided among Lucille, Eula, and Robert Jr. It appeared that Neema's hunch had been correct and that Margaret had died as a child. Lucille was now the sole surviving child. The last ledger that Sarah shared with Neema traced the most recent tax payments. The current owner of the Harper property was listed as Constance Newman, Lucille's daughter. It appeared that Lucille deeded the property to her when her health had begun to fail. Neema was ecstatic. She had found the link to the real information she needed. She excitedly copied Constance's address and phone number.

Neema couldn't think of anything else she could accomplish in Pope City until she could arrange to meet Lucille, so she decided to head back to DC the next day. Driving back to the motel, she considered how best to contact Constance. Although she had a phone number, she thought that a "cold call" would be disconcerting. A letter seemed more appropriate, and she began writing drafts in her head as she drove. The tone had to be just right – not too direct, too personal, too wordy, or too presumptuous – but it had to catch Constance's attention.

Back at work, Neema wrote Constance a letter in longhand on her State Department letterhead. It read:

Dear Ms. Newman,

My name is Neema Washington. I live in Washington, DC and work for the federal government. I have included a photo and my resume. My mother, Lily Washington, died a few months ago. Before she passed, she told me that I was related to Robert and Ruby Harper, your grandparents.

I just returned from a visit to Pope City where I learned that their oldest daughter, your mother, Lucille Harper Johnson, is alive and living with you. I would love to talk with both of you if you are willing. Please call to let me know a good time for us to talk. I can be reached at (202) 727-1111, ext. 75.

Sincerely,
Neema Washington

The much-anticipated call came two weeks later. Neema tried to start with small talk, but Constance got right to the point.

"How are you related to my grandparents?"

Neema decided to be as straightforward as Constance. She told her about Lily's insistence that the Harpers were her grandparents and how she had deduced that Robert Harper, Jr. might be her father. Constance didn't interrupt. After Neema's ten-minute monologue, Constance snickered sarcastically.

"Uncle Junior? That's what we called Robert Jr. You wouldn't be the only outside child Uncle Junior had. Mama says he was so good-looking that women chased him all the time."

Although she was clear that Constance had just made a disparaging remark about her mother, Neema didn't respond.

"How's your mother doing?"

"She's hanging in there. Mind is sharp as a tack. She's living with me and my husband now. She's frail and uses a wheelchair, but otherwise she's doing okay. What did you say your mother's name was?"

"Lily Washington. She was married to Joseph Washington. His daddy was pastor of Payne Chapel."

"I'm sure Mother would remember him." Constance promised to call back after she talked with Lucille.

Neema was delighted, but when weeks passed and Constance hadn't called, she began to worry. Just as she was thinking that Lucille might not want to talk with her, Constance called. She said that her mother had immediately perked up when she mentioned Lily's name.

"My mother is naturally nosy, but she asked more questions than usual about you and your mother. I think something about your call knocked her a bit off-kilter, but she said you should come see her if you're ever this way."

Neema wasn't about to miss this opportunity. "As a matter of fact, I will be in Atlanta for a meeting next week," she lied. "Do you think I can drive down to Pope City to see her?"

Constance agreed but warned Neema, "Mother's tough, but please don't upset her."

* * * * *

A week later, Constance met Neema in the lobby of Pope City's Holiday Inn to take her to meet Lucille. The first thing Neema noticed was that she and Constance didn't share a family resemblance. She must look like her father, Neema imagined. Constance appeared to be four or five years older than Neema, in her early 50s. She was pleasant but didn't smile easily.

"Mother is anxious to talk to you," Constance said as they drove, and she laid out the rules. "You have one hour. When I stand up, you'll know it's time to leave, even if Mama objects. Oh, one more thing. My mother is known to be crotchety, says what's on her mind, interrupts often, and dismisses other people's points of view. It's just who she is."

Constance's home was beautiful. The sprawling brick ranch with a two-car garage sat on what looked like an acre lot. The manicured yard was ablaze with azaleas, hydrangeas, roses, camellias, and crepe myrtle trees. Lucille was sitting in her wheelchair on Constance's large screened-in back porch. Neema immediately saw the family resemblance. Lucille looked like an older, darker version of her! Except for their complexions, they shared the same aquiline nose, thin lips, and naturally wavy hair. You wouldn't know Lucille was 82 by looking at her face. She didn't have the saggy neck or wrinkled, blotchy skin that you might expect on someone her age. Black don't crack, Neema thought. Lucille was thin but not sickly looking, and Neema could tell that Constance took good care of her. Lucille was dressed in expensive cotton jogging pants, a long sleeve t-shirt, and walking shoes.

Lucille gave Neema the once-over and said nothing as Neema fumbled through her obligatory Southern greeting.

"It's so nice to meet you, Miss Lucille. I feel blessed to have this opportunity to speak with you. How are you doing? I hear you're 82 years old. Hard to believe! Why, you don't—"

Lucille interrupted. "You look like my Daddy, Robert Harper. He was half white. White folks who didn't know him thought he was Jewish. You got that white folks' coloring. Yeah," she chuckled, "you favor him, all right. Funny how that resemblance thing pops up from one generation to another. Knowed your other granddaddy, too, Rev. Washington. We's two of the best families ever lived in Pope City, the Harpers and the Washingtons."

Constance pulled up a chair to sit between Neema and her mother. Lucille leaned over and told her to go back in the house. Constance frowned but didn't object. Apparently, she had learned from experience that crossing Lucille was not a good idea.

When Constance was gone, Lucille turned her head and stared at the stunning flowers in Constance's yard. "That girl can grow just about anything. Got that from me and my mama."

"My mother was very fond of your mother. Talked about her all the time during the last month of her life."

"I bet she did!" Lucille sucked her teeth. "My mama liked Lily more than she did me. Always Lily this and Lily that. Wish your mama had stayed outta our house."

Neema was taken aback. She hadn't had any reason to think that Lucille might hold bad feelings toward her mother.

"Constance, say you think my brother was some kin to you. Why you think that?"

Neema repeated the story about Lily's end-of-life revelation that Rev. and Mrs. Harper were her grandparents. The only way that could be true was if their only son, Robert Jr., was her father.

Lucille twisted up her mouth and shook her head from side to side.

"Lawd, child," she grunted, "you got the story all figured out wrong. Junior won't your father, and Lily won't your mother."

"What?" Neema practically screamed. "That's crazy. Miss Lucille, I don't understand. What are you saying?"

"I'm saying that Lily ain't your mother and you won't born in no Africa. You was born on the southside of Chicago. My grandma, Ada May Peabody, delivered you in her house all by herself. When you was a week old, Lily come by and picked you up and ran off to Africa. And don't go thinking I'm your mama. Everybody thought I would show up with a swollen belly and no husband on account of my being the darkest child. But it won't me."

"Well, who was it then?" Neema demanded. "Eula? Margaret? Who is my mother?"

"I'm through wid it. Done talkin'." Lucille folded her arms across her chest to make her point. "Me and my sisters promised Mama and Poppa on a stack of Bibles that we'd never tell a soul. Took pity on you when Constance told me 'bout you, but I'm through wid it. Done said too much already."

"Well at least tell me who my father is. If it's not Robert Jr., is it Joseph Washington?"

"Honestly, child, you know everything you need to know to be at peace in the world. Your mama told you the truth, and I'm tellin' you 'xactly the same thing. You the granddaughter of Robert and Ruby Harper. You got Harper blood. Be proud of that and stop askin' questions. Your parents are the people that raised you and loved you, Lily and Joseph Washington. Nothing else matter. Now go on back home, Nita."

"My name is Neema, Miss Lucille. N-e-e-m-a."

"Neema? What kinda name that is?"

"African. It means grace."

"Grace?" Lucille raised her feeble voice and laughed so loudly she scared Neema. "Mama sho named you. She sang and moaned 'bout grace from mornin' to night. Grace. Amazing Grace. Lucille sang softly, "Amazing grace how sweet the sound that saved a wretch like me."

* * * * *

Neema felt nauseous and asked to use the bathroom. She couldn't make sense of what she had just heard. What kind of person would tell someone that her mother was not her mother? And then suggest that her father wasn't either of the men she thought he might be? Miss Lucille must have dementia.

Constance knocked on the bathroom door. "Mama's tired," she said. "I think it's time for me to take you back to the motel."

Neema collected herself and walked back onto the porch. After Neema had mumbled a less than sincere thank you and said goodbye, Lucille gestured for her to bend down.

"Don't you worry none," she whispered. "I just need some time to pray and see my way through this. Lord's gettin' ready to call me home, so I gotta get straight with the Master. No more secrets. No more lies. I'll let you know when the Lord tells me to talk with you again."

Neema returned to the motel, barely able to process that her mother was not her mother and her father not her father. She couldn't process the horrific news. That evening, she called Rose in desperation.

"Rose, I don't know who my mother is or my father. I don't think I can survive this. None of this makes sense!" They talked and cried most of the night.

The next morning, Neema left Pope city and returned to DC.

* * * * *

Six months after her meeting with Miss Lucille, Neema was feeling more desolate than ever. She wasn't sleeping, couldn't concentrate at work, didn't have any ambition – just couldn't get her old rhythm back. Her therapist suspected that she had a more serious problem than finding her rhythm, and Neema eventually admitted to taking "uppers" like Ritalin and Librium to get through the day and "downers" to sleep at night. Drugs were easy to get in DC. Her therapist suggested she take an extended sick leave and check into a private outpatient mental health facility where she could receive intensive daily treatment. Neema refused. She told her doctor that she couldn't be away from her job even if she wanted to. The real reason, which she didn't share, was that she was worried someone at work would find out.

As Neema was preparing to leave her office one spring day in 1996, she did one last check of her voicemail messages and was pleasantly surprised to hear one from Constance.

"Hi, Neema. Listen, Mama's worrying me about you. She's insisting that you come and see her. Claims the Lord won't call her home until the two of you talk. Of course, Mama is always thinking the Lord is about to call her home, so I don't think there's any real rush. I don't know what's going on, but I thought I should let you know."

Neema jumped up from her chair, twirled around, threw up her arms, and quietly rejoiced. Finally, she thought, I'll get the answers I so desperately need.

* * * * *

Neema flew to Atlanta, rented a car, and took the familiar 100-mile drive to Pope City. When she arrived at Constance's home, Constance took Neema to Lucille's bedroom. Lucille's health had deteriorated some since Neema had seen her six months ago. Large dark circles under her eyes overshadowed the rest of her face. Her mouth was slightly twisted and Neema assumed she'd had a stroke until Lucille spoke in her normal, commanding voice.

"Glad you made it 'fore the Lord called me home. Why you sittin' so far away? Move that chair closer.

Ain't gonna bite you. You know, dyin' ain't scary like folks make it out to be. The Bible say I'm goin' to a happy place where I'll be with my family. You believe that, Grace?" Neema nodded dutifully. "But I ain't gonna be able to put on my long white robe and see my folks if I don't lay my burdens down like it say in that song. You know what song I'm talking 'bout?" Lucille hummed a few bars. "Grace, what's the name of it? Won't come to me now."

"*Down By the Riverside*, Miss Lucille." Neema thought it best not to correct Lucille's confusion about her name this time. At least she remembered what it meant.

"I know why you come here," Miss Lucille continued. "You wanna know who your mama and daddy was. You don't know this, but Poppa didn't know who *his* daddy was, and it was a source of hurt for him his entire life. Chile, you even worse off. You don't know who your mama *or* your daddy is. I called you back 'cause I don't want you to go through life with the kinda pain Poppa had. I could already see it in your eyes the last time you was here. The hurt you holding on the inside showin' up on your outside. I want you to heal, but you gotta listen to the whole story. That's the only way you'll find some peace. By the way, I ain't Miss Lucille to you. I'm your aunt. Call me Aunt Lucille."

Neema felt comforted by Lucille's words. "Okay, Aunt Lucille," she said softly, "tell me the whole story. I'm ready to know everything about my family."

Lucille reached in her nightstand and pulled out an 8x10 framed picture of Rev. Robert and Mrs. Ruby Harper. She handed it to Neema.

"That's Mama and Poppa," Lucille said. "Don't know when the picture was took, but it musta been some special occasion 'cause they all dressed up and standin' in front of the fireplace in the livin' room. We almost never got to go in the livin' room. Mama kept all her nice things in there and was very particular about them. Ain't they a beautiful couple?"

Neema stared at the faded picture of the two strangers whom she now knew were her maternal grandparents. They didn't exactly look like a couple. He was bald, could pass for white, and wore round, wire-rimmed spectacles that gave him a studious look. His suit stretched over his slightly protruding stomach, but otherwise he looked to be thin. The collar of his white starched shirt had been perfectly ironed. Ruby was dark-skinned, heavy-set, and several inches taller than her husband. She wore a beige taffeta dress with a lace bodice and matching long-sleeved jacket and a pearl choker and earrings. Her netted pillbox hat seemed too small for her full, pleasant face. Ruby held a two-strap leather pocketbook in one hand and long cotton gloves in the other.

"Us Harpers wasn't like yo Mama's high-class people. Mama said Lily's folks come from free Negroes who went to college, owned banks, preached in big churches, and bought fancy clothes up North. But Grace, those folks is just one part of who you is. Can't be whole without knowin' the other part."

"The Harpers always had a tough row to hoe. Went through every kinda pain and suff'rin' that white folks could dish out. My great grandparents on Poppa's side, Jim and Harriet Martin, was slaves, purchased on an auction block right here in downtown Pope City. They worked on the Martin plantation, where they picked cotton from "can see to can't see" six days a week. All the men, women, and chillin who picked cotton had quotas and worked from July to early fall under the scorching Georgia sun."

Neema thought back to her brief visit to a cotton field during her first visit to Pope City.

"Cotton pickin' ain't easy," Lucille explained. "I know. When I was a teenager, I picked cotton on Poppa's farmland. I was the oldest child, so Poppa would made me go wid him and the other farm hands. Those cotton burrs use to cut our hands something fierce, and the cocklebur weeds and sticky briers would stick to our skin like leeches. Then there was the boll weevils, mosquitoes, gnats, and snakes. It was tough! I would cry so hard that Poppa had to stop takin' me out to the fields. Can't imagine what it was like back in the day for those slave folk. And the poor women! After workin' all day, they had to be bothered with some nasty white man tryin' to have their way wid 'em."

"Lincoln signed the freedom papers, but them crackers wouldn't let our folks leave. For two years, my great grandparents stayed on the Martin plantation. Instead of being slaves, they was called sharecroppers, but ain't nothin' really changed. Then the government come round talkin' 'bout givin' Great Grandpa Jim forty acres and a mule. Well, ain't no land or mule ever showed up. Poppa said his granddaddy would tell him all the time, 'Boy, go git my forty acres!' Then he would turn and wink. 'And don't forget my damn mule!'"

Lucille laughed as if she was hearing the joke for the first time. She lingered on the memory for a moment before she continued.

"My Grandma Sarah was a sharecropper, born in my great grandparents' shack. She and Granddaddy Jeff Harper had four children they could barely feed, and then they had Poppa."

"Poppa must have been one surprise! He was the whitest colored baby I suspect folks ever seen, and this must have made Poppa feel left out because his sisters and brothers was dark-skinned. Granddaddy Jeff took one look at him and left for Detroit. Grandma Sarah ain't never seen him again. She knowed that there won't no way she could sharecrop without a man, and she knowed that a half-white baby would send courtin' men running like jackrabbits. So, she did what she had to do and split up her family. She took Poppa and his two older sisters to live in her mama's shack. The two oldest boys stayed with her to help farm her sharecropper piece of land."

"Grandma Sarah didn't find a man and couldn't make ends meet, so she decided to use the one gift God gave her. She was a natural root healer. Could pick the right plant to cure whatever ailed you. So that's how she made her money. For chest and head colds, she'd take beef tallow from dead cows, mix the white fat with turpentine, rub it on your chest and neck, and then wrap you up with sackcloth she warmed over a potbelly stove. Grace, you talk 'bout stanky! I ain't never smelled nothin' so awful in my life. But it sho' nuff worked. When she got old and couldn't stoop down or see too well, she'd take me out in the woods to help her. She walked real fast-like, carried a long stick, and would point at the plant she wanted. If I picked the wrong one, she'd bless me out. She'd also bless you out if you said she won't no real doctor. Sarah Harper was a pistol, all right. Folks didn't mess with her either. I can see why she and Poppa didn't get along. They bumped heads all the time."

"Ada Peabody, my other grandma, the one that delivered you, saw her uncle's body swingin' from a pine tree. Scared her so bad, she and Pop Louis run away in the middle of the night to Chicago. They'd heard stories 'bout how things was so much better for colored folks up North, but they found out that Chicago had the same kinda crackers there that they'd left in Georgia!"

"When Poppa got to be eighteen, he left home. He didn't know where he was goin' but he knowed he had to leave Grandma Sarah's house. He took a job thirty miles away. That's where he met Mama. She was standin' in front of her church, and Poppa said she was one good-looking chocolate woman with her long wavy hair and big legs. Mama was just sixteen when they married."

Lucille closed her eyes and seemed to be falling asleep.

"Miss Lucille let's take a break," Neema suggested. "I'll be back tomorrow. I'm getting a little tired myself from travelling all day," she lied.

"Suit yourself, but I ain't through talking. Come back tomorrow," Lucille instructed.

Neema didn't go straight back to the motel. Instead, she decided to visit the graves of Robert and Ruby Harper at West End Cemetery. By the time she found the cemetery, the sky looked like a storm was threatening. The sprawling, hilly cemetery was overrun with scraggly bushes, dead looking trees, piles of leaves, broken vases, and dirty plastic flowers scattered on top of sunken graves. No one was around, and the nearby utility shed appeared vacant. The cemetery looked like a scene from a horror movie.

It took Neema half an hour to find the side-by-side graves: Rev. Robert L. Harper 1892-1970 and Ruby Harper 1896-1972. Neema sat on a large boulder near the graves and reflected on what she has just learned from Aunt Lucille. Her knowledge of African American history was extensive, but today was the first time that she could connect the dots between her life and slavery. Lily had been proud of being a descendant of free Negroes. Joseph had suspected that his family had once been enslaved but didn't know for sure. Now Neema had names and places for her newly discovered enslaved ancestors. Neema tried to process all that she had learned but couldn't. It was too much, and she was exhausted. Trapped in a tug of war between "want to know" and "don't want to know," she returned to the motel and had a hard time falling asleep.

The next morning when Neema arrived at Constance's home Lucille seemed more alert.

"Where did I leave off yesterday?"

"You were talking about your grandmother, Ada Peabody."

"Oh, my. I ain't talked about Grandma Ada in a real long time. She my grandma on my mama's side. Lived up the road from us. In 1919 when I was six, Grandma Ada come bustin' in our house so upset she could barely get her words out. She said that in the middle of the night, white men dragged Uncle Eddie Lee out of his house, took him in the woods, ripped all his clothes off, and strung him up on a tall pine tree. Yes, they did. Claimed he killed a white man over some white woman they was both courtin', but all the colored folks say won't so."

"When things quieted down a bit, Poppa and Mama went up there to check on our kinfolks. All the colored people stayed in their homes. Didn't go to the store, church, work, school, not even the honky-tonk because they was scared they be lynched, too. People said the white folks, including white ladies and chillin, stood around and watched the hangin' – laughin' and talkin' while they collected Eddie Lee's clothes and parts of his body for trinkets. The sheriff didn't say a mumblin' word. Nobody arrested. Won't long after that lots of colored people left the county and never came back, including Grandma Ada and Pop Louis. They packed up all their belongings and headed for Chicago. Course they wanted all of us to go wid 'em, but Daddy won't buyin' it. Know what Daddy said? 'Can't see no difference 'tween crackers in the South and crackers in the North.'" Lucille chuckled.

"Poppa was right. Few months after Grandma Ada and Pop Louis moved to Chicago, a colored boy went swimmin' in that lake they got up there and accidently crossed over to the white folks' beach.

Some of those evil white crackers threw rocks at that poor boy's head and knocked him out. Boy drowned and ain't no one ever went to jail for the killin'. But them white folks in Chicago went crazy for four days. When it ended, they say more than a thousand colored families lost their homes, and a lot of coloreds was kilt. Can you imagine? Lawd, have mercy. They was so many race wars up North the summer of 1919 they called it Red Summer. By the grace of God, our folks stayed safe."

"Grace, I bet you think you done heard the worse 'bout our family. Well, you ain't. Hold on while I tell you about Daddy's brother, Uncle Jake. Jake wasn't like the rest of the family. He never went to church or 'sociated with Christian people. He stuttered, but he liked to talk all the time. He had a mouth on him, always arguin' bout somethin' and then nothin'. Just mostly hung out in honky tonks, foolin' 'round with fast women, drankin' moonshine liquor, listenin' to gut bucket music, and gamblin' with jokers with big plans and no money. 'Jake just got a bad itch he couldn't scratch,' Grandma Sarah use to say. One night, the same summer Grandma and Pop Louis left for Chicago, Jake caught a hobo train to Birmingham. He found a decent job and a room in the colored part of town, but that wasn't enough. Jake couldn't stay away from the wildlife. One night, he stumbled and fell off the sidewalk, landed in a ditch, and passed out. When he woke up, he was in a paddy wagon for just bein' drunk in the street and was put away for thirty days of hard labor in a convict camp. Grace, back in dem days white police picked up colored men for no reason at all, like being drunk and not having a job. Uncle Jake spent a month workin' in an underground hellhole. One day, a former church member saw Jake roamin' the streets of Birmingham with no arms and no place to stay. He sent word to Poppa, who went to Birmingham and brought Uncle Jake back home."

"I can't forget the day Poppa come back from Birmingham and helped Uncle Jake out of the back seat. I was in the yard by myself and thought I would pass out when I saw Uncle Jake with no arms below his elbows. The half arms hung from his shoulders, and the scarred, stitched up elbows was covered with pus and welts. Had good home training and knew not to stare at infirmed people but couldn't take my eyes off him. His face was almost as scary. His wild, nappy hair, mustache, and beard was going every which- a- way. Poppa told me to get Mama and the other chillin. Mama and my sisters and brother come out and started hollering. Never forget it."

"Poppa told Uncle Jake to tell all of us what happened to him. Said we needed to hear what white folks do to colored people and pray that no one in the family would ever have to go through the same. I can picture this in my mind to this day. Jake said he and the other colored men slept on stained cots full of vermin in an underground coal mine where they worked from dawn to dusk. Nothing to eat but biscuits, corn pone, salt meat, and cold beans. I seen hard times, Grace, but can't 'magine this."

"No, this is horrible, and I—" Neema tried to add her two cents, but Lucille cut her off.

"Uncle Jake and the others rode little train cars under the ground pulled by mule teams. The men had to crawl on their knees through tunnels, lay down on their sides, and dig coal with picks. But Jake was blessed. He learnt to handle the mules, and white folks gave him that job. One day, when the little train car stopped on the track, Uncle Jake crawled under it to fix it. The mules heaved forward, and the train car cut off both his arms from the elbows. They patched him up and dropped him off in front of the Negro church 'cause he won't no good to nobody no more. After that, Uncle Jake just roamed the streets, beggin' for food and liquor 'til Poppa brought him home."

Lucille was getting ready to continue when Constance came out on the porch.

"Mama, your lunch is on the stove. While you eat, I thought I'd take Neema to Poplar Springs to see the old house and show her around the old neighborhood. Think I'll stop by Miss Lovie's. What you think?"

"Well, I guess it won't do no harm. But don't go to Lovie's empty-handed, and don't be takin' her none of those nasty store-bought cakes."

* * * * *

Constance and Neema stopped at Ruthie Mae's Café to order a take-out dinner for Miss Lovie. While they waited, they decided to sit and have a cup of coffee. It was the first opportunity they had had to have a casual conversation.

Constance apologized for her initial, less than warm welcome. She explained that her sisters had moved away, one to Ohio and the other to

California, so she was her mother's primary caretaker and was very protective of her. She said that both she and her husband were teachers at the local public high school. Before Lucille's health began to decline, they had enjoyed traveling to visit relatives and taking fishing vacations in Pensacola, Florida. They had two married children who lived in the North.

Once back on the road, it was less then fifteen minutes before Constance announced that they had arrived in Poplar Springs. Neema felt like she was in a time warp. Poplar Springs was literally a ghost town. The unpaved streets were framed by gullies that held stagnant rainwater. Vacant, barely standing houses lined the four streets that comprised the small neighborhood. Stray dogs roamed the street, and cats slept on rotting porches, some ironically adorned with beautiful potted plants. Neema didn't see a single poplar tree.

Constance stopped on the side of the road near the entrance of a long gravel driveway.

"We're here," she said pointing, "my grandparents' house. My sisters and I spent a lot of time here while our parents were at work. Mama was a maid in a private home, and Daddy worked in the mill. After school, we'd walk over here and stay until Daddy picked us up. I have such fond memories of this house. I wish you'd known my grandparents. They were angels in our lives."

"At every family reunion, the old folks would tell stories about our family's history." She smiled, reminiscing. "We heard those stories a million times, but never got tired of listening to them. The stories always ended with the charge, 'Don't you young folks ever forget, okay? Never forget!'"

As they sat in front of the long driveway in front of the old Harper house, Constance told Neema the story of how Robert Harper had turned his family's fortune around.

"I think Mama told you that Granddaddy left home when he was 18. He landed a job in a cotton mill cleaning toilets and mopping floors. Back then, Black men couldn't get the higher paying carpenter or machinist jobs. He got a lucky break, though, when one of the white carpenters fell through a temporary floor and broke his leg. Granddaddy helped rescue the man and repair the floor, and the boss was impressed with his work. He hired him as a carpenter's helper and gave him a raise. Granddaddy began to notice that all the white carpenters had outside jobs doing repairs, renting out houses, and selling property. He had a knack for business, so he listened closely when they talked about their outside projects so he could learn the business of fixing and selling houses. After years of steady employment at the mill and pinching every penny he could, he bought and remodeled the house down this driveway, our home house. The three-bedroom house had a kitchen, indoor bathroom, living room, dining room, and screened-in front and back porch. Pretty soon everyone was asking Granddaddy to work on their houses on his days off. The family was finally financially stable."

"In addition to his job in the cotton mill and his carpentry business, Granddaddy acquired an unexpected third one. He became a minister. When

Grandma Ruby, a staunch church-going woman, complained about his inconsistent church attendance, Granddaddy started going regularly. Over time he got more and more involved in church life, becoming a trustee and then a lay minister. Eventually, he was called by the Lord and was ordained in the AME church. He was assigned to a small church in the county. Grandma was delighted, and from the day he was ordained until the day she died, she called her husband Rev. Harper."

Constance and Neema got out of the car and walked down the driveway. The newly painted facade failed to disguise the obvious – the wood frame house would soon be beyond repair. After taking it all in for a minute, they began to circle the house and Constance continued talking.

"It's not much to see now, but back in the day our grandparents had one of the best-looking houses in Poplar Springs. There was a gigantic chinaberry tree in the front yard, and bluebirds, robins, and thrushes would sing as they pecked at the chinaberries that fell to the ground. The finishing touches were Grandma Ruby's beautiful flower and vegetable gardens. That really set it off from the other houses. The people we have renting take pretty good care of the place and basically pay their rent on time. My sisters and I had wanted to tear the house down, but Mama wasn't having it. And you've been around my mother long enough to know that she gets her way."

Neema was surprised by how much she was enjoying Constance's description of their family home. Constance said that her Grandmother Ruby's flower garden had been in the side yard and that its inviting aromas, rainbow colors, and dancing butterflies had brightened the drab and gritty neighborhood. The sweet smell of yellow honeysuckle vines used to hug the trestle that their grandfather had built and blended harmoniously with scents of sweet peas, four o'clocks, roses, lantana, and jasmines. Miss Ruby's elephant ear plants had been the size of elephant ears, she claimed. The fenced-in vegetable garden in the back had been home to a fig tree and rows of collards, turnip greens, tomatoes, green beans, okra, and peppers. Neema could just imagine all the great meals they had provided.

When they reached the back door, Constance called out.

"Miss Charlie Mae. Miss Charlie Mae? Are you in there? You got company."

Miss Charlie Mae surely weighed at least 250 pounds. She waddled to the screen door and yelled, "Ya'll come in. Don't tell me Wilbur didn't pay the rent this month!"

"Don't worry," Constance said lightheartedly, "you're caught up. Just stopped by to show our out-of-town company our old home."

Neema noted that Constance didn't refer to her as her cousin. After minutes explaining to Miss Charlie Mae that they had just wanted to say hello and didn't have time to "sit a spell and talk," Neema and Constance walked back to the car to continue their tour of Poplar Springs.

"There used to be some real characters in Poplar Springs when we were growing up, but Grandma Ruby never had to worry about keeping an eye on us. The whole community kept trouble away from us and us out of trouble." Constance suddenly had a memory that made her laugh. "Would you believe we had a Sunday school teacher who was illiterate? Sure did! Miss Cooper. Lived next door and was one mean old lady, the neighborhood chief of police. It seemed like she was always peeping over her raggedy fence hoping to catch one of us misbehaving. Miss Sis across the street would sit on her porch dipping snuff and entertain herself by insisting that every time a child passed her house, no matter how often, they had to greet her. Walk by without a proper 'Good afternoon, Miss Sis' and you'd have to listen to a fifteen-minute speech on manners!"

Neema noticed a huge magnolia tree sitting in one of the small yards.

"Wow, what a magnificent tree! I love the way they smell," Neema said.

"That's the Grant house," Constance explained. "Some of the family still lives there. Their grandmother is dead now, but back in the day she was *always* in the yard sweeping up leaves. That magnolia tree would drop big crunchy brown leaves from sunup to sundown, so the yard never really looked swept. But everyday Grandma Grant would get out there with her rake, seemingly unfazed that the leaves she had raked up yesterday showed up the next. Either her mind was a little off, or she was a glutton for punishment!"

Neema thought the story was hilarious. When they finished laughing, Constance continued the tour.

"Let's go down the road here. I want to show you Ku Klux Hill. Any Black child who dared go up there had a whipping in store if their parents found out."

To call the place a hill only described the physical attributes of the unimpressive mound of soil, patchy grass, and scraggly trees. Constance explained that when she was growing up, once a year hooded and robed Klan members would line up their cars and drive around Pope City honking horns and waving Confederate flags. The point was to deliver a message to the Black community: Stay in your place, or you'll end up swinging from a tree. The parade would end at night with a torch rally on Ku Klux Hill, where the masked cowards would burn a twelve-foot-high cross. For the city's Black people, that hill represented a mountain of terror and fear.

"Neema, this hill is how white folks kept our family from achieving the American dream. The Harpers were on our way, but white folks have a way of letting you know when you've stepped out of your place. Whether it's 1900 or 1995, DC or Pope City, if you have a million dollars or no dollars, they let you know when you've gone too far. We're going to go see Miss Lovie now. I'll let her tell you what happened to our family."

According to Constance, Miss Lovie was a tamer of African hair, a pipeline for all information, and one of the most respected women in the community. She knew all the credible news as well as the brazen gossip, and she had a fine-tuned sense of timing about what, who, and when to tell. She was 94 years old now, but in her twenties, she had started a Depression-proof business – Black women would give Miss Lovie their last dime for her to slather Royal Crown grease on their wooly hair and rake a hot comb through it. Having that scorching metal comb inches from your face tended to make her clients very compliant and agreeable, and so she enjoyed her work. She also enjoyed being the sieve that filtered the news about disobedient children, marital indiscretions, and sightings of strangers, be they Black or white. Most importantly, Black housekeepers shared information about their white employers in Miss Lovie's beauty parlor.

Miss Lovie had never left Poplar Springs. Her granddaughter's family lived with her now and took care of her. Neema, becoming increasingly familiar with how small-town Southerners went visiting, watched Constance climb the steps and knock on the unlatched screen porch door.

"Hello, anybody home? Miss Lovie, it's Constance!"

Neema was surprised to see Miss Lovie open the screen door. Although she was bent over and hard of hearing, Miss Lovie was mentally sharp. She thanked Constance profusely for the chicken dinner from Ruthie Mae's Café – said it was a real treat to get a restaurant meal – and instructed her granddaughter to put it in the refrigerator. After catching up on how Miss Lovie and her family were doing, Constance introduced Neema, this time as a family member. When they had settled down comfortably in the living room, Constance asked Miss Lovie if she wouldn't mind telling the story of how the Klan terrorized the Harper family.

"Don't mind one bit," Miss Lovie said. "I remember it like it happened yesterday. It was 1925. I was 24 and Lucille was a teenager. This very house you sitting in backed up to a house owned by a white man that he rented to some colored people. First day of each month, he'd come to pick up his rent money. One evening he knocked on my door and told me that my fence was on his land and ordered me to knock it down. I gave that cracker a piece of my mind. Told him I got land papers to prove it. I rolled my eyes at that rascal, turned around, and slammed the door. Well, we kept quarrelling, me and that cracker, and I told your granddaddy, Reverend Harper, 'bout it. Like I knew he would, he called on all the men in Poplar Springs to keep watch over me. I told folks around here not to worry 'bout me because I won't scared of white folks. I worked for myself. Ain't never had to clean their nasty houses or wipe their ugly babies' behinds. I figured the mean cracker would let me be."

"Well, I was wrong. One night the Klan busted in my house after I got in bed, tied me up, dragged me out my house, and dumped me in the back of a pickup truck. They were planning to take me to Ku Klux Hill. Lucky for me, my neighbor heard all the noise and saw what happened, and he ran to tell Reverend Harper. The reverend got dressed and sent word for all the men in Poplar Springs to meet at his house and to bring their guns. A procession of four, maybe five cars and trucks filled with some real mad Black men headed for Ku Klux Hill. When they got there, they walked up to the white men with their guns drawn. Reverend Harper demanded they let me go." Miss Lovie let out a sigh and then gave a devilish smile. "Those stupid, drunken Kluxers saw they were outnumbered and ran away! It was the best thing ever happened to me. I swear I wouldn't be here today if it hadn't been for Robert Harper. But he not only saved my life, he saved the lives of all the peoples around here in one way or another."

Neema was really moved by all the stories she was hearing about the Harpers and happy to know she was part of such a fine family. She was also glad she had gotten to know Constance, who she decided she liked.

The next day when Neema arrived to see Lucille, she was waiting on the porch, eager to take up the story where Lovie had left off.

"What happened wid her and the Klan stays wid me even after all these years. Good thing Lovie or Poppa didn't get strung up that day, but the Klan eventually did chase Poppa out of town. Not too long after Lovie's kidnappin', one of the maids in Poplar Springs who worked for Klansman heard him talkin' 'bout stringin' up Robert Harper. Poppa said he won't scared of no crackers, but he decided to leave because he didn't want us to be in any danger. So, he caught the next train to Chicago and stayed with his in-laws, my Mama's parents, Ada and Louis Peabody. The night he left, Mama packed his bags, laid out his best Sunday clothes for the trip, and fixed him a dinner basket. Me and Mama tried not to cry in front of the younger chillin, but we couldn't help it. Everybody cried."

"Poppa won't impressed with Chicago, the so-called land of milk and honey. People livin' stacked up on top of each other or in houses so close to each other you could smell what yo' neighbor was cookin'. No yards or gardens, just a few spindly flowers stuck in dirt-filled coffee cans set on concrete steps. No one seemed to be watching the chillen, who was running up and down the streets yellin', fightin', and dodgin' cars. Decent, God-fearin' folks lived next door to whorehouses and whiskey joints. The stockyards was nearby, and Poppa said the smell of slaughtered cows, pigs, sheep, and burning animal hair made his stomach turn. Back home he was used to early to bed, early to rise, but in Chicago police and ambulance sirens wailed all night, and streetlights shined in his window bright as the sun."

"Poppa picked up enough carpentry work to give some money to his in-laws for room and board and send some to Mama. After six weeks of misery, he was ready to come home and prayed for the courage and strength to defeat any threats he might have to face from the Klan. His prayers was answered in the most unimaginable way."

"Pop Louis worked in one of the stockyards and got a kick outta tellin' the men he worked wid how Uncle Jake lost his arms in the convict camp. One of Pop Louis' buddies told him he knowed a former stockyard worker, a white guy, who lost his arms in World War I and got fake wooden arms and metal hook hands from the Army. Ain't no one ever heard such a thing! Pop Louis and his buddy asked 'round and found out that the man wid the fake arms was dead but his widow still lived in the city. It musta been the Lawd's work cause the white widow woman agreed to see Pop Louis and my daddy."

Constance jumped in to give a little history.

"During World War I, the army produced prosthetics for armless soldiers returning from the war. The wooden arms bent at the elbow and ended with metal claw hooks for hands that could hold and manipulate things. The prosthetic was attached to a harness that strapped around the amputee's shoulders and behind his neck. It allowed veterans to take care of their daily hygiene, cook, feed themselves, and, in some cases like the widow's husband, get jobs. The widow gave Granddaddy and Pop Louis the device. Said it didn't make sense to keep the wooden arm if another man could use it."

"Grace," Lucille said, "I can't tell you how happy we was when Poppa come back home. What a glorious day! He said the trip North revealed a scripture to him and it's still the family's favorite verse. You need to remember this. It's from Genesis 50:20. 'Man intended to harm me, but God can turn evil into good.' Poppa preached from that verse a lot. He said he thought he was runnin' 'way from the Klan in Pope City but really he was runnin' to Chicago to get his brother's arms."

"After Poppa returned, us Harpers flourished. Uncle Jake learned to use his new arms well enough to make a livin' with a mule-drawn vegetable cart. Poppa picked up where he had left off – workin' on his real estate business durin' the week and preachin' on Sundays. He also started up the Harper Construction Company. At first, he just had fo' workers – Coochie, Sage, Popeye, and Dookey. They was a raggedy bunch that drank too much on the weekends, but under Poppa's supervision they did pretty decent work. As his bizness growed, one of the first things he done with his money was buy forty acres of farmland and several mules – a way of honorin' his granddaddy."

Neema was still enjoying hearing all the memories, but she was beginning to wonder if maybe Lucille had forgotten what she really needed to know. This was her third visit in a row and they still hadn't gotten to the most important topic. Neema used Lucille's brief pause to ask.

"Aunt Lucille, will we be talking about my mother soon? Now that I've learned so much about my new family, I'm more anxious than ever to know who she is."

"Hush, Chile," Lucille said, "I'm gettin' to that. Let me tell the story my way. Let's see, where was I? Oh, yeah, Poppa had come back and his bizness was goin' good. Then two years later, we had another reason to celebrate. That was 1935. I was a grown woman and low and behold, Mama and Poppa going to have another baby! Margaret was what they called a late baby. Mama was old and didn't carry well. Sad to say, Margaret was born too soon, a real tiny baby. To make things worse, her bottom come out before her head. By the time she was six months, we all knew somethin' won't right 'bout her. She didn't crawl or reach for things like babies do. But people loved to look at her because she was a beautiful chile, real light-skinned with wavy hair. People teased Mama that she had outdid herself and saved the best for last."

"Margaret had trouble learnin' and never did grow up like other chillin. She could say a few words but didn't talk much. Folks started whisperin' that she was feeble-minded and wondered how such a pretty chile could be cursed like that. But we loved Margaret and never treated her no different. She was a happy child, and we was proud to have her in our family."

"Me, Eula, and Robert Jr. was near 'bout grown, but we'd play with her and take her to the store to get penny candy. She loved candy. One day in 1948, when Margaret was fourteen, we couldn't find her. She always stayed close to home and, when she disappeared, we knew somethin' won't right. Daddy and me found her ten hours later in a ditch in the woods on Ku Klux Hill. Oh, Grace, I can still see this picture in my head. Margaret was tied up, bloomers stuffed in her mouth, and dress rolled up under her breasts. Blood was dripping between her legs. She had been raped but thank God she was alive. The white sheriff come to the house and took some notes but never come back. Margaret got worser after this. She never talked much before, but after this rape, she didn't talk at all. I won't telling you the truth the last time you was here. We know who raped yo mother and who yo daddy is. It was the white man who owned the store in Poplar Springs where we bought candy. We called him Mr. Ed. Grace, I do not know what his last name was."

Lucille told Neema that the storeowner's customers were mostly Negro children in Poplar Springs. The store had nothing in it any adult would want to buy. He sold Nehi and Coke drinks from a large ice chest and barely edible penny treats, like melting lollipops stuck to cellophane wrappers, candy cigarettes used to practice smoking, unchewable Bazooka bubble gum, and Mary Janes that refused to dislodge from teeth. Margaret loved to visit the store with her siblings. When Rev. Harper picked her up out of the ditch, her right hand was closed tightly. She was clutching a nickel she probably found on the ground and was headed to Mr. Ed's store. The family had no idea Margaret could find the store, but she did.

The neighbors always had their suspicions about Mr. Ed. A forty-year-old bachelor who was too familiar with young Negro girls. He engaged them in small talk, showed them card tricks, and juggled balls in the air. Adults knew something wasn't right about slimy Ed and warned the girls not to go to the store alone.

A few months after the attack, Ruby noticed Margaret was not having a period but decided that she just needed time to heal. Then, the Harpers' worst nightmare came true. Fourteen-year-old Margaret was pregnant. When Ruby wrote to her mother, Ada Peabody in Chicago, Ada convinced Robert and Ruby that she could take care of Margaret and the new baby until things settled down. Mama took Margaret to Chicago on the train and left her with Grandma Ada.

"Grace," Lucille sighed, "yo mother Margaret died in Chicago in 1949 while birthing you. Yo great-grandmother Ada buried her in Chicago. Mama and Daddy agreed to let Lily, who was already in Gary, take you to Africa. You was just a few weeks old."

Neema wept uncontrollably. It was all too much. She was the child of a special-needs, 14-year-old mother and a white racist rapist! She regretted ever going down this path.

Lucille reached out and held her hand.

"Don't cry, Grace. Don't be like my Grandma Sarah, lettin' regrets and sorrows weigh you down. Take a lesson from yo' Granddaddy Harper. Poppa didn't never let the situation he was born into map out his life. He let go the pain and bitterness of fightin' for his mama's love and wishin' for a daddy. When your granddaddy died, he was at peace with the world. He had played the hand he was dealt and played it well – a successful family man, businessman, community leader, and man of God. And who woulda thought that all his grand babies would go to college! And that Margaret's daughter would turn out to be the smartest of them all. Lawd, I sure do wish Mama and Poppa coulda knowed you. They woulda been so proud. Ain't God somethin'? It's like our family scripture say. 'When men intend to harm me, God can turn this evil into good.' Grace, you the good that came from an evil act."

Neema returned to DC with a lot to think about. She still couldn't wrap her head around the fact that Lily and Joseph weren't her birth parents, but relieved to finally know the truth and the history of her new Harper family. Two weeks after she left Pope City, she got a message from Constance. Lucille had died peacefully in her sleep on Mother's Day, 1996, exactly two years after Lily.

CHAPTER SEVEN

WASHINGTON, DC

Neema's state of mind when she returned to work at the State Department was predictable. She had difficulty focusing on the stack of work and phone messages on her desk. Adding to the stress, Laura, her secretary, directed her attention to an interoffice memo from the assistant director of African Affairs requesting an update on the West African Women's Entrepreneurship Initiative. Neema panicked. She had totally forgotten the assignment's upcoming due date.

Neema felt ill and asked Laura to cancel her afternoon appointments and hold all telephone calls. As she stared out her office window, she envisioned her life zooming by like a movie in fast-forward. She was a toddler playing with Aunt Eni at Makola Market in Accra, a ten-year-old bowing before an admiring Nashville congregation, a teenager having a heated discussion with her mother about Jack and Jill, a high school senior trying to decide between

Fisk and Howard, a love-struck young woman in bed with Nigel in his off-campus apartment.

"What's wrong with me?" she thought.

Neema decided to pack up her things and work from home. The movie in her head continued as she walked to the Foggy Bottom Metro train station. She heard Aunt Lucille's voice as she imagined the scene of her fourteen-year-old mother's rape – hands behind her back, panties in her mouth, blood between her legs, and a nickel clenched in her delicate hand. Neema had taken a few steps off the curb to cross the street when she realized that the pedestrian walk signal was red. She tried to backstep quickly to the curb but it was too late. She felt an excruciating pain race through her body, and then she blacked out.

When Neema opened her eyes, the pain was gone. She was swimming underwater, searching for seashells at Labadi Beach in Accra. Men were singing their tradition Twi fishing songs while they pulled their nets out of the water. She was surrounded by a school of butterfly fish with fins that looked like the wings of butterflies. A school of mackerels circled over her head, and Neema laughed as she fanned them away. The amplified sounds of the waves were familiar and calming. A bright, blinding light emanated from the ocean's floor, and she heard her mother and father singing a line from *Amazing Grace*, "I once was lost but now I'm found." In the distance, they were standing under a baobab tree, beckoning her to come closer. They were happy and holding hands. As she stepped forward to join them, she turned around at the sound of a familiar voice. It was Nigel. "No, Neema," he was saying, "don't go. Stay with me."

Neema opened her eyes to discover yet another strange place. The first thing she saw was an IV drip. She was lying in a narrow hospital bed. She had an oxygen mask on her face and some kind of contraption on her right leg. When she propped herself up on her elbows, she could see a catheter bag hanging on the side of her bed. She called out for a nurse and frantically looked for the call button. When the nurse responded, she explained to Neema that she had been hit by a car and then went to find the doctor.

"Good afternoon, Miss Washington," the doctor said as he walked into the room. "I'm Dr. Walker. How are you feeling?"

Neema hunched her shoulders to indicate she didn't really know.

"I understand," he said. "You're in the Intensive Care Unit at George Washington Hospital. You got hit by a car yesterday while you were crossing the street. You've been heavily sedated for two days in the Intensive Care Unit here at George Washington Hospital to prevent you from moving during scans, MRIs, and surgery. We attached a fixation device to your broken right leg. The surgeons drilled holes in the undamaged part of your leg and secured the fractured part to it. Good news. No permanent damage to your neck and spine. With rehab and therapy, in due time, you will be fine."

"Where are my Mother and Daddy? Nigel? They were all here."

"Miss Washington, the worst is over."

"But my parents and Nigel were here," Neema insisted.

"It's not unusual to hallucinate during life-threatening accidents like you experienced. It's like the mind must help the body escape to a better place and time. These episodes even have a name, Near Death Experiences or NDE. But, for now, let's concentrate on your healing and rehabilitation. You are cleared for visitors. Call your family and friends now. Let's concentrate on your healing and rehabilitation."

Rose, Vanessa, Vickie and a few of her other friends visited her in the hospital. When Neema called her cousin Christine in Little Rock to let her know what had happened, she wanted to come to DC right away. Neema convinced her not to come yet because she might need her when she came home. Seven days after the accident, Neema was transferred to the Potomac Rehabilitation Center for thirty days of therapy, five days a week, four hours each day. At her request, her treatment included psychological counseling.

Responding to the doctor's advice, Rose created a schedule for evening and weekend visits from Neema's Mojo Club and Sankofa Theater friends. They brought food and decorated her room with flowers and artwork. Her secretary Laura visited occasionally to keep Neema up to date about things at work, and her supervisor lessened her worry by assuring her that her responsibilities would be taken care of until she was ready to return to work.

"Rose," Neema asked, "did you put Jamal on the visitors list?"

Rose hesitated. "Neema, let's talk about Jamal later. It's your call, but you need to think about this some more before you decide to contact him."

The exhausting therapy routine included exercise bikes, treadmills, resistance bands, aquatic exercise, massage, and ultrasound stimulation. Her sessions with her psychologist, Dr. Christy, were equally draining but insightful and therapeutic. With no outside distractions, Neema was forced to face the anguish and insecurity she had felt most of her life. The sessions helped her resolve the feelings she had as a child about her parents' separation, the life altering event that had led to her attachment anxiety and fear of commitment. Dr. Christy also helped her explore what Aunt Lucille had said about finding the other half to be whole. She now understood that she could be proud to be both a Harper and a Washington.

When Neema was a little more than halfway through her 30-day stay at the rehabilitation center, she had to undergo physical and psychological evaluations. Her physical therapists gave her high marks. She had progressed from wheelchair to robot-assisted gait training to a regular walker. Dr. Christy was also pleased with Neema. She handed her a tape recorder and a notebook.

"Neema, I'd like *you* to evaluate your progress. What have you learned about yourself these past couple of weeks? What insights are leading to healing and a path forward? You can record your thoughts or write in the notebook. Take your time. There's no deadline."

Neema took the materials back to her room and not so gently threw them in the drawer of her nightstand. But the question – what have you learned about yourself? – kept her awake at night. After a few days of self-reflection, apprehension, and some fear, she began to write.

Dear Dr. Christy,

To be honest, I was not pleased about this assignment. I am comfortable giving advice and solving other people's problems, but not so good at looking myself in the mirror and asking, who are you? what are you feeling? My sessions with you have been enlightening. Thank you so much.

Unlike most people who have only two sets of grandparents, I accept that I have three, the Harpers, the Washingtons, and the Robinsons. My ancestors' lives are stories of both privilege and oppression, and they share much in common. All three family trees are rooted in amazing grace, unimaginable resilience, hard work, unrelenting faith, and optimism. I have a remarkable heritage and feel a responsibility not to disappoint my family or myself.

I am the biological daughter of Margaret Harper, but Joseph and Lily Washington are my parents. They loved me and did the best they could in a number of complicated situations. And I was fortunate to be able to thrive in Ghana, in Nashville, and at Howard University – communities that sheltered me from the racism that so many in my family experienced.

When I really take a long look in the mirror, I am always shocked to see my mother, Lily Robinson Washington. I know that I paid more attention to my father because he was easier to love and protected me from my mother's demands and criticisms. But I am definitely more like my mother. Like the book title, "My Mother, Myself" is an apt description of who I am.

Like Lily, I left home to get away from a controlling mother. My insistence on attending Howard, a college I knew little about and had never visited, was all about getting away from her. When I fell in love with Nigel and introduced him to Mother, she didn't like him, just as her mother hadn't liked my father. My insistence on continuing my relationship with Nigel was much like Lily moving to Africa with my father. And when he betrayed her trust, she ran away to Nashville, just like I ran back to Ghana when Nigel betrayed me.

I can see now how I became a fast-track, never-look-back, goal-obsessed person. I was driven by lost love and self-pity. That was how Mother tried to heal, by focusing on her career and showing the world how smart she was. But many of the traits I copied from her haven't served me well. I can be unreasonable, controlling, and dismissive, and whether consciously or unconsciously, I believe that men cannot be trusted. They will eventually disappoint you or break your heart.

Therapy has helped me to understand that I am not Lily Robinson Washington, or Joseph Washington, or the ill-fated offspring of a mentally disabled teenager and a white rapist. There is no pre-ordained blueprint for my life. No DNA traits or characteristics from my biological or adoptive families can ever fully define me or confine me. My life's work is to define myself for myself. This is a tall order that I will continue to work on in therapy.

This is the first of many entries in my new journal as I continue to explore your question, "What have I learned about myself?"

* * * * *

Jamal called frequently to ask when he could visit, but Neema was taking Rose's advice. "I don't think the time is right," she'd explain.

Whether or not to see Jamal was a complicated and agonizing decision. He was good company in and out of bed, and a smart brother without an inflated ego. At times, Neema saw their casual arrangement as a win-win for her. She had all the perks of good sex, stimulating conversation, and great companionship without any of the hassles. No man was asking her what she was cooking for dinner or to take his underwear out of the dryer or how much she was spending on clothes. At other times, she was lonely and visualized waking up with Jamal on a lazy Sunday morning. He would make coffee while she toasted bagels. They might spend the rest of the morning listening to jazz and reading *The New York Times* and *The Washington Post*. In the afternoon maybe they'd take a walk to Dupont Circle or the National Mall. Neema knew that these musings were nonproductive, so she used skills learned in therapy to shut down "what if" moments.

One afternoon, Neema, on her walker, entered her room after a water therapy class. She had been concentrating on being sure her walker cleared the door threshold. When she looked up, Jamal was standing in front of the window. She was so taken aback that she thought she might be hallucinating, an adverse reaction to one of her medicines, perhaps. They had not seen each other for over a month, and Neema had to contain her impulse to scream his name in glee. Jamal was the first to speak.

"Hi, Neema, how you doing? It's so good to finally see you! I've really missed you."

He made an attempt to hug and kiss her, but the walker proved a formidable barrier. He awkwardly brushed her cheek with his hand, stroked her arm, and kissed her forehead. After they exchanged pleasantries, Jamal brought up the subject of them continuing their relationship.

"Baby, I can't wait until you get out of here. You mean so much to me. Life isn't the same—"

Neema cut him off. "Look, Jamal, our relationship is over."

"Aw, come on, Neema, I know you've been through a lot with your family and now the accident. I want to be with you, help you get through all this. We can take our time and work out our relationship."

"How much time are you thinking about, Jamal?"

"You know my situation. I'm in a bad marriage, but I can't just pack my bags and move out. The kids are just thirteen and nine, and—"

"And what, Jamal?" Neema had sat down on the bed. She was scowling. "Let's do the math. I'm forty-six years old. By the time your youngest kid goes to college, I'll be fifty-five. Jamal, I've learned one undeniable lesson recently. Life is both precious and unpredictable. I'm not waiting for anything anymore. I'm restarting my life now, and I need more than you can offer."

For the first time, Neema saw another side of Jamal. The articulate, analytical, well-read problem-solver was at a loss for words. When he had composed himself, his tone changed.

"Look, Neema, you're the one who defined the boundaries of our relationship. You told me that you didn't care that I was married, said you didn't want to know anything about my wife or children. Correct me if I'm wrong!"

"Well," Neema said, "that was then and this is now. Goodbye, Jamal."

* * * * *

At the end of her thirty-day treatment, Neema left the rehabilitation center. Her mother's first cousin Christine flew from Little Rock and stayed with her until she was well enough to return to the office. Neema was happy to see her friends Rose and Vanessa give Christine a break and take her sightseeing and to nice restaurants.

By the time Neema went back to work, she had decided to follow her father's advice: "Stay focused on your dreams." As a first step, she threw the box of birthday cards from Nigel into the trash. She didn't need reminders of the love she lost. She had a life to live.

She still liked her work at the State Department but was angry that she was passed over for the assignment she had wanted in Ghana. She realized, though, that there was another way she could live in Accra like she'd always wanted. She would apply for early retirement and move there. Over the past twenty years or so, she had traveled there often for both business and vacations. She loved the landscape, the sounds, the smells, and the people. And she knew lots of State Department people there, so she wouldn't be lonely.

Weeks later, she found three envelopes on her desk – one contained the forms she had requested from the Federal Employees Retirement System, one was marked Official US State Department, and the third was marked Official Business Jamaican Embassy. Of course, this last one would be the annual birthday card from Nigel and so she tossed it aside. She opened the letter from the State Department. To her surprise, it said that she had been nominated for the post of Deputy Chief of Missions at the US Embassy in Accra. Finally, a position in Ghana! Neema was ecstatic, but now she had a dilemma – should she take early retirement and leave the stress of work behind, or take the embassy position? She was happy that the long Labor Day weekend would give her some time to think.

Neema had her eye on the Deputy Chief of Missions position since she had first started working at the State Department. She sat at her desk at home and methodically listed the pros and cons of taking the job. The pros were easy. She'd be the number two diplomat in Ghana, responsible for the day-to-day management of the political, educational, economic, and public affairs sections of the embassy. The promotion was noteworthy, particularly for a Black woman, and the pay increase was a compelling bonus.

The list of cons was more complex. She got up and went to the kitchen to make a cup of tea. Leaning back against the kitchen counter sipping her tea, she wondered what she would miss if she left DC. Of course, she would miss Rose and her outings with the Mojo nightclub sisters and Sankofa Theater pals. DC, "Chocolate City," was an exciting urbane setting with lots of activities like concerts at Carter Barron Amphitheatre, picnics in Rock Creek Park, and tons of festivals, museums, and art exhibits. With the help of her therapist, she had ideas for getting out more, perhaps joining a book club, a gym, a travel club for singles, or doing volunteer work. She also wanted to reconnect with Faye, her friend from college. It seemed strange to be thinking about leaving the country just as she was contemplating all the fun things she could do here, especially in retirement.

There were other things to consider. As chief of mission, Neema would have an apartment in the embassy compound. She had stayed in the embassy's guest apartments many times when she was there on official business, but now the compound would be her home. Would living there mean she would be on duty 24-7? It was also the home of many of the other embassy staff members and might be like living in the dorm at Howard. Would she lose her privacy?

Also, moving to Accra would end her therapy and perhaps her healing. She had made notable progress and felt better physically and emotionally but doubted she would find a suitable therapist in Accra. Which led her to consider the biggest issue – what was her real motivation for leaving? Was she still running from the pain of losing Nigel? She decided to sleep on it.

The next day Neema took a long walk. By the time she'd gone one block, she was pretty sure that Nigel was *not* the reason she wanted to go to Ghana. The next block, she thought that *maybe* he was why she wanted to go. By Tuesday, she realized that she couldn't work through this issue by herself, and she made an appointment to see her therapist. The session was revealing, forcing her to admit that, at least in part, she was running from Nigel to a romanticized Accra. But if she didn't take the job and instead retired, what would she *do*? She had twenty years of service but was only forty-six years old.

Neema needed to take a break from planning her life. She sat at her desk and worked on finishing some routine paperwork she had brought from the office. Midway through the stack, she picked up the sign-off sheet for a proposal that had won a sizable grant to work with the Ghanaian government on an AIDS and clean water community development project. Neema was pleased. The grant had been awarded to Harris and Associates, an African American consulting firm. She had pushed the State Department to cast a wider net to get more grant proposals from minority firms.

Suddenly Neema had an epiphany. She knew many of the CEOs of these minority companies and often interacted with them at conferences and meetings. They frequently made overtures about wanting to hire her "when you get tired of those people at the State Department." It was a perfect solution. She would retire, take a year off to avoid conflict of interests, and then let her contacts know she was a free agent. As an independent consultant, she could stay in her beloved condo and choose the projects in Africa that she wanted to work on. During her year off, she'd travel with On the GO, a Black singles' group. She was looking forward to touring countries she'd never visited like Bahia or Cartagena.

When she returned to the office, Neema wrote to her direct supervisor declining the promotion and giving notice of her intent to retire. Next, she started filling out the twenty-page federal retirement packet that she had received. It gave her an instant headache and took two days to complete. Neema finally turned her attention to the mounds of paperwork that had accumulated on her desk. It was a few days before she ran across Nigel's card. She tossed it in the trash, but then couldn't help herself and retrieved it. She sighed as she opened it.

Dear Neema,

I have sent you birthday cards for twenty years, hoping that you would respond. I had heard that you were married and so I tried not to write anything inappropriate. You respected my decision to marry Edith in 1969 and never attempted to contact me. I tried to respect your marriage as well. I only recently learned that you hadn't married.

I have been divorced for 10 years and can't seem to stop thinking about you. We are both getting older, and I can no longer live with this pain. Howard's homecoming is next month. Please see me if only for the last time. I'll be waiting at our usual spot, the steps of Founders Library. The game is on October 12th at 1:00.

I never stopped loving you. Nigel

The letter brought up so many conflicting emotions and Neema chastised herself for reading it. At the same time, she knew she had to resolve her feelings about Nigel and his betrayal. Maybe meeting him at Howard would help. Or maybe it would make things even more painful. She didn't know. Suppose I meet him, she thought, and he turns out to be a pompous ass. She was picturing him as the fine 21-year-old brother she had dated, but people change. Maybe he's fat and balding now. Neema stared at herself in the full-length mirror. I've changed, too, she thought. I look like someone who got hit by a car! And if I go, what should I wear?

What should I do with my hair? And how do you greet a former lover after 26 years? Do we hug?

"Stop!" Neema said to her reflection. She realized that she was reverting to her pre-therapy behaviors – obsessing about things she couldn't control, planning her life instead of enjoying it, trying to predict and avoid life's inevitable disappointments, and fretting about pointless matters, like what she should wear. She sat down and exhaled. Like a divine revelation, Neema remembered the advice her father had given her during her sophomore year in college.

"Neema," he'd said, "matters of love take circuitous twists and turns. Stay focused on your dreams, and the right man will find you."

It was time to see if her father was right. On Saturday, October 12th, Neema hailed a cab. "Take me to Howard University."

About The Author

Jackie Jordan is an education writer who loves to travel and research her family's genealogy. During a time of loss and grief, Jackie discovered the power of creative writing and has been writing ever since. Creative writing has given her language to construct new worlds through prose as well as forge new pathways for personal healing and growth. This book is her first novel.